STRIKEFAST

Simon Larren's latest mission for British Counter Espionage is a dangerous trip over the Afghan-Soviet border to rescue a double agent from a mental hospital in Samarkand. But ex-diplomat Nevile Mannering has changed sides more than twice and now his loyalties are unreliable. Despite the help of Caroline Brand and a young Afghani named Sharif, Larren's mission soon becomes a confusion of disasters, dangers, and sheer bad luck — and through it all he is pitted against the ruthless Soviet KGB.

ROBERT CHARLES

STRIKEFAST

Complete and Unabridged

LINFORD
Leicester

First published in Great Britain

First Linford Edition
published 1998

British Library CIP Data

Charles, Robert, *1938*–
    Strikefast.—Large print ed.—
Linford mystery library
1. Detective and mystery stories
2. Large type books
I. Title
823.9'14 [F]

ISBN 0–7089–5286–0

Published by
F. A. Thorpe (Publishing) Ltd.
Anstey, Leicestershire
Set by Words & Graphics Ltd.
Anstey, Leicestershire
Printed and bound in Great Britain by
T. J. International Ltd., Padstow, Cornwall
This book is printed on acid-free paper

1

Kabul

Afghanistan, the melting pot of the ancient world. Here was the crossroads for a score of marching civilizations. Here the arid, savage mountains had witnessed the conquering advance of every empire from that of Alexander the Great of Macedonia to that of Queen Victoria of England. Here the Mongol hordes of Ghengis Khan and Tamerlane had raped and burned and plundered, sweeping all before them from the violent north. Here the Caliphs of Persia and the Mongol emperors of India had in different periods of time imposed their iron rule. Here the grumbling, sweating, swearing soldiers immortalized by Kipling had fought and cursed and died to maintain the furthest frontiers of the British Empire. For Afghanistan it had been the last empire, for after the retreat of the British the well-trodden, blood-soaked land was now an independent kingdom. The bleak mountain passes no longer echoed to the resounding tread of invading armies, no foreign despot rules by force and oppression, and the heart of Asia rested from the swirl of world affairs in one of the few tranquil moments of its history.

Yet how long that period of tranquillity would last was any man's guess. History had an infallible habit of repeating itself, for the leaders of men were all too ignorant of the lessons of history. The ancient invasion routes through the mighty barrier of the Hindu Kush and the Khyber Pass that had served the war lords of old were obsolete in a modern age of jet aircraft, for now there were giant armouries of nuclear missiles that could straddle and devastate the world with such speed and on such a scale that the wholesale butchering by Ghengis Khan and Tamerlane would rate as just a drop in an ocean of blood by comparison. However, even though the passes had lost their strategic military value, Afghanistan was still not the peaceful and forgotten backwater of Asia which perhaps she deserved to be. As a neutral buffer state between the Soviet Union to the north and the conflicting spheres of western interest in Pakistan and India to the south and east, and Persia to the west, Afghanistan was now subject to much more subtle pressures.

The modern empire builders came not with fire and sword, but with smiles and theodolites. And they came not as warriors of a rampaging war lord, but as servants of a political doctrine, either Democracy or Communism. They no longer built empires but sought to widen their spheres of influence, or to restrain each other, which they fondly believed was a different and more honourable aim. Their methods were to build rather than to destroy, and so Afghanistan was infiltrated by American and Russian engineers, busily constructing roads and schools and hospitals. It was a vast and beneficial improvement on the crude onslaughts of Ghengis Khan and Tamerlane, and the optimists with no knowledge of the endless pattern of history could even hope that the end result would not be the same.

With the technicians and the engineers there came a liberal sprinkling of spies, for espionage and intrigue enjoyed a new vogue in the modern process of conquest. The world had widened, yet paradoxically, because of the new jet speed of transport and communications, it had also contracted. There were too many eyes and ears and voices for the forces of conquest to march boldly and openly in daylight. Instead they had to wait for one of the interchangeable propaganda words of 'aggression' and 'defence' to give a seemingly valid cause for advance, and in the meantime the power struggle was conducted by silent, unknown agents in the dark. America and Russia were both strongly represented in Afghanistan, but after the crumbling of her empire Great Britain showed only an occasional flicker of interest in her former territory. Such a flicker of interest was being shown now as the airliner in which Simon Larren was a passenger descended over Kabul airport.

4

★ ★ ★

Larren was a tall, sombre man, silent and unsmiling. He had very little to smile about. He had no immediate family and an absolute minimum of friends. Nature had created him for the role of a lone wolf, and fate had completed the process. His parents and his only sister had all died together when Hitler's bombers had blitzed London in 1944, and the lost happiness of a brief marriage many years later had again ended in violence with his wife's death. There had been no one since Andrea, at least no one important. Now he was alone. His features were stamped with a hard, lean jawline and jet black hair, but most noticeable about him was the strange grey-green colour of his eyes. They were the eyes of a hunter, of a man who still possessed the animal ability to enjoy a kill. But Simon Larren was not a sadist. Instead he ranked with the kind of men who found a compulsion to climb mountains, or to stalk wild beasts in the jungle on equal terms. There had to be

5

a strong challenge, equal or preferably unequal odds.

There were few places in twentieth-century society where he could have found a home, but after Andrea had died he had found his place. A wise man knew that to catch a thief it was best to set a thief, and to kill a killer it was best to send another killer. That was why Simon Larren had proved invaluable to British Counter Espionage.

His present mission was not specifically to kill and was somewhat outside the normal field of counter-espionage operations. In fact, if secret agents had unions there would probably be a who-does-what strike staged by the men of MI5. Fortunataly secret agents did not have trade unions, and as lower department levels rarely knew what their own members were doing, much less those of their co-existing rivals, many operations could often overlap, either by accident or design. Counter Espionage was composed of full-backs, while MI5 provided the centre-forwards, but this time Larren was far ahead of the divided team. His Whitehall controller had a personal interest in this job, which was why Larren had flown with BOAC to Tehran, and then with Ariana Afghan Airways to Kabul.

A very dilapidated taxi conveyed him from the airport to the city where he booked a room in the modern Spinzar Hotel. He had not expected to find central heating, hot and cold running water and private baths in Afghanistan, but the Spinzar could provide all three and he was able to get cleaned up and change his clothes before he descended into the streets.

Kabul was a city crushed between the hostile shoulders of two aggressive mountains, on their slopes tiny houses balanced precariously, like square concrete pill-boxes, while the city itself spread out more widely in the valley to the north and south. The Kabul river ran straight through the middle, but now it was a shrunken trickle that belied the flowing torrent of Kipling legend. It smelled as though the whole of Kabul used its banks as one great outdoor lavatory, and after making the mistake of a closer inspection Larren realized that that was exactly what was happening. Afghanistan was still relatively primitive, despite the Spinzar Hotel.

There was an atmosphere about Kabul, smoky and conflicting. There were a few cars and some brightly painted lorries in the streets, but there was also a line of plodding camels with strange, sack-shrouded burdens. There were modern buildings, but they were far outnumbered by narrow mud-walled streets where homes and shops were dark, cave-like holes. There were men in smart western suits but mostly there were men in large turbans, with shabby jackets and long shirt-tails flapping outside their trousers. The only women he saw were shrouded from head to toe in a strange hooded robe that made them look like grey or black zombies as they glided along the darkening pavements, but there were very few of them compared to the vast number of men strolling the streets. Women still had no real freedom of movement, and were kept very much indoors.

It was getting dusk now, and to the south-east the sky was coloured a dark, smoky red by the sunset. Smoke was very much in the atmosphere, from the braziers of the kebab stalls and from the wood fires that were being lit all over the city to combat the night cold. Larren turned up the collar of his overcoat and walked swiftly northward, past the guarded walls of the Royal Palace. Ahead stretched a broad avenue lined by maple trees, and far away in the distance there was just enough light to silhouette the forbidding ramparts of the Hindu Kush.

It took him three-quarters of an hour to find the place he wanted. It was a large building constructed around a small central courtyard, situated to the right of the main avenue. Once it had been the home of some relatively wealthy Afghani, but it was now sub-let into six different apartments. There was no name plate of any kind beside the open gateway to the courtyard, but this was the only building in the area which fitted the description he had been given in London and Larren went inside. He stood for a moment, noting that one of the paved flagstones was broken. No one came to question his presence and finally he turned to the flight of outside steps that led up to the second-floor balcony that encircled the three sides of the courtyard. He knocked quietly on the door of number four, and after a short wait it opened.

They stared at each other, and after a moment Larren offered one of his rare smiles. It was a long time since they had last met, far away in the Caribbean, but he had known who to expect while she had not. He said calmly:

"Hello, Caroline."

"Simon Larren," she said it at last, slowly. "Well I'll be damned. You'd better come inside."

Larren accepted the offer and she closed the door behind him. It was a sparsely furnished room; a table covered by a blue chequered cloth, a few chairs, rugs, a bookcase with very few books, and a large coloured calendar on one of the cream-painted walls. Two closed doors led beyond, presumably to a bedroom and a kitchen. The electric light made it look clean and bright but it was not a home. There was nothing personal or permanent about it. Larren turned with his hands still in his overcoat pockets and faced Caroline Brand.

She had not changed much over the intervening years. The deep blue eyes were just as he had remembered them, but now she wore her hair longer so that the luxuriant, dark gold waves just touched to her shoulders. She still favoured pink for the loose-knit roll-neck sweater she wore over a dark skirt, and he noted that the skirt was longer and more modest than she usually preferred. Perhaps because Afghanistan in November was so much colder than the Caribbean, but more likely because of the strict moral climate.

"Smith might have warned me," she said at last. "I knew that someone was due to arrive tonight, but I didn't expect to see you."

Larren had a brief mental picture of their employer sitting in his book-lined Whitehall office, a man as unassuming in appearance as in name. For all practical purposes Smith would be indistinguishable from any other pin-striped and bowler-hatted slave of the city. It was only the undetected powerhouse of mental energy that made him what he was. Smith had a brain like an ice-cold computer.

Larren said: "You should know that Smith never makes an unnecessary introduction. He won't even let his left hand know what his right hand looks like, much less what it's doing. If I was to be brainwashed by the KGB tomorrow there are about six names that I could betray, but no more. That's just the way our chubby little boss wants things kept. Your name is already one of the six, so you are no more compromised than you were before."

She said warily: "I don't particularly like the sound of that."

She watched him take off his overcoat, and after a moment's hesitation came forward to take it from him and fold it neatly over a chair. When she straightened up again and turned to face him they were standing close, and his hands closed lightly over her shoulders. He smiled and said quietly:

"Caroline, you were not quite so reserved the last time that we met."

Her face was unresponsive until he kissed her, and only then did her blue eyes close and the stiffness ease out of her body. It was a momentary relaxation, and he tactfully pulled away when he sensed her resistance strengthen again. He asked casually:

"Tell me, do you still wear that tiny little double-barrelled palm gun just below your navel. The one you used to save my life on San Quito?"[1]

She smiled then, a little sadly, and pushed his hands away from her shoulders.

"Simon, that's none of your business, not any more. Smith separated us after the San Quito job because he knew that we had become lovers. But we didn't really need Smith to make that decision. If you remember we had decided even

[1] See *The Fourth Shadow*

before we returned to London that it was no good. I was fond of you, Simon, but we both knew that it couldn't last. It's still no good. And if we start again it still won't last. Between two people with a job like ours it has to be sex, not love, and I don't want to start it up again."

Larren watched her face for a moment, but he didn't argue because he knew that she was right. Caroline turned away from him and went into the kitchen. He heard the clink of glasses as she continued in the same calm tone.

"You used to drink scotch, but I'm afraid I don't have any. It's difficult to get out here. The best I can offer is American bourbon. I got that through a friend."

"That'll do fine."

He waited until she brought the glasses. The rye whisky was a shade lighter in colour than her hair, and he made a small toast.

"To old times."

She smiled. "I think the present would be easier without those memories."

She drank, and then leaned back so

14

that she was half-sitting against the edge of the table. Her fingers toyed with her glass and she regarded him gravely.

"Simon, I said before that I don't like the sound of this job. When you appear it usually means that Smith anticipates violence. And if we are working together again to prevent you from compromising any new faces then there must be a very strong possibility that you *will* finish up by being brainwashed by the KGB. My feminine intuition tells me that we are both being pushed into the front line, and rated as semi-dispensable."

Larren's mouth curled faintly.

"Your feminine intuition could well be right, for me at least. I'm definitely expected to stick my neck out." He paused. "You'd better tell me how much you know, and then I'll fill you in with the rest. What was your briefing?"

Caroline said wryly: "Not very informative. As you know we don't have a resident local agent in Kabul. That's basically why I am here. A sort of short-term substitute. My briefing was simply to establish myself here with a good cover, to make myself familiar with the city, with the customs and the language. In short to fit myself to provide a base, a line of contact, and the local knowledge that would normally come from a permanent agent on the spot. I've been here for three months now, working six days a week in the British library and doing all the rest in my spare time. I know that I'm out here as an advance scout for some kind of operation, but the exact nature of that operation is something that you'll have to explain."

Larren said quietly: "It's very simple. Do you recall the case of Nevile Mannering?"

Caroline said slowly: "I remember. No one capable of reading news headlines with two-inch lettering could forget. Mannering was a top British diplomat who vanished into the Soviet Union three years ago seeking political asylum. It was also rumoured that he was one of our own department, an agent who turned double and then had to get out fast and run to his new masters."

Larren said wryly: "The truth isn't even that simple. Mannering wasn't a double agent, he's more of a treble. In actual fact he's still one of Smith's agents. He's been inside the Soviet Union for just over the three years now, and it's only recently that he's dared to make a single communication back to Smith. How the word got through I don't know, the source is something else that Smith doesn't want compromised. Anyway, the word is that Mannering has accumulated a mass of mind-stored information, and now he's ready to pull the real double-cross and come out. At the moment he's being treated at a nursing home on the outskirts of Samarkand. He's either suffered or feigned some kind of a mental or nervous breakdown. The important thing is that he's within reach, just a mere two hundred miles beyond the Afghan-Soviet border, and it's my job to go in and get him."

Caroline stared at him very dubiously and he added:

"This particular joy-ride has been honoured with a code-name. Rather appropriate too because it's the only way that the job can be done. The word is *Strikefast*."

2

The Man from the CIA

Caroline stared at him for almost a minute, her blue eyes searching his face, and then she drank the rest of her bourbon and said:

"If Smith really wants to make a gift of your head to the Russians, why doesn't he wrap it up in pretty paper with holly and berries, tie it up with pretty pink string, and then post it to Moscow for Christmas? It would be so much simpler."

Larren said calmly: "I think you may be under-estimating my abilities. I may be sticking my neck out, but I intend to take good care that it doesn't get chopped off. The job should only take a matter of days; a quick dash across the frontier, snatch Mannering, back again, and then the next flight out of Kabul. Speed and surprise should enable me to get away with it."

"And what's my part in all this?"

"Limited, which should make you happier. Once I get under way you're going to fall sick, a bad cold or stomach trouble, anything that's an excuse to shirk that library job for a few days and stay here by the telephone. As soon as I get back into Afghanistan I'll give you a call, just the code-name and my estimated time of arrival in Kabul. Then I want you to book me two seats on the first available international flight to New Delhi. I'll leave you my passport, and the one we've made up for Mannering. The entry visas into Afghanistan are okay, mine's genuine, Mannering's is forged, but you can't tell the difference. Exit visas from Afghanistan are not necessary, and travelling with British passports there'll be no visa formalities at all in India. We can relax there until we can get a BOAC flight to London."

He paused, and then added: "You'll stick around for a few days, and then wind up your job at the library and come home; say that your mother has died in England, or something similar.

It's best that you don't leave directly with myself; and Mannering, just in case there's a last-minute hitch."

"And what happens if there's a first-minute hitch? If you fail to return to Afghanistan and there's no phone call."

Larren said grimly: "Give me four days from the moment I cross the frontier. This operation has to succeed fast or it won't succeed at all, so if you haven't heard from me after the four days are up, then that's your signal to get out even faster than I went in. Even if I get picked up immediately I should be able to hold out for those first few days. Then I'll scream my head off, just as anyone else would do under modern interrogation methods, so don't hang around after the time limit." He smiled and added: "But I don't really anticipate getting caught."

Caroline watched him finish his bourbon, and then said bluntly:

"It all sounds just too easy. But Nevile Mannering isn't exactly a stick of candy — and the KGB aren't exactly the gurgling and cooing little people who win prizes at baby shows. In practice I don't see how you're going to carry off this one-man cavalry charge."

"I'm not making a one-man cavalry charge. I'm expecting some local help." He came forward and set his empty glass down upon the table close to her hip, still looking directly into her eyes. Caroline Brand was a very lovely young woman, the old memories stirred, and there was a temptation to let his hand stray and linger on her thigh. He quelled it partly because of her earlier rejection of their old relationship, and partly because this present job needed the complete dedication of all his time and thought. It was a pity, but he continued:

"According to my briefing you should be in contact with one of our American cousins from the CIA. They are pretty plentiful in this part of the world, and should be able to provide me with a good Afghani agent to guide me across the frontier. I must have a front-man who can speak the language."

"So that's it," Caroline said softly. "I wondered why that contact was made. But if you're expecting wholehearted co-operation from that direction you'll be out of luck. Our American cousin didn't like making that contact one little bit. Even my charm and beauty failed to impress him."

"But he made the contact?"

She nodded. "He came into the library, very reluctantly. Smith had warned me to expect him, but I didn't know why. He'd been ordered to make the contact but he didn't know why either. He was hostile about it. He doesn't like working in the dark. And he didn't believe in my innocent ignorance of what was happening. He expected answers from me, and was very dubious when he found that I expected answers from him. Now it seems that you're the mysterious cause behind it all, and somehow I don't think he's going to love you for it."

Larren found another smile for that. "Nobody loves me anyway, and I'm too old to shed tears. The important thing is that the contact is made. When can you get him here to meet me?"

"He may not want to meet you."

"He didn't want to make the initial

contact, but he did. So don't worry about it. Tell him it's safer if he comes to me. I don't want to know any more about him than I have to. What I don't know I can't reveal to anyone else. He'll appreciate that aspect. If he doesn't want to come here, tell him that he can choose a neutral ground. I don't mind."

Caroline hesitated, and then said:

"He'll come here. He's been before." She interpreted his gaze and explained coldly: "I told you that he expected answers from me. I hoped that the answers would come from him, and as we couldn't talk openly in the library I invited him here."

"I see. How quickly can you get him here again?"

"I should be able to get in touch sometime tomorrow, so probably tomorrow night. If he wants to play?"

Larren said calmly: "He'll play." He picked up his empty glass again and changed the subject. "It wasn't exactly scotch, but it's damned cold out there and I'm more vulnerable than a brass monkey. So how about one for the road?"

An hour passed before Larren finally departed from Caroline Brand. By then the temperature had dropped to freezing and the night was bitterly cold. He walked briskly back to the Spinzar Hotel, said a sincere prayer of gratitude for the central heating, and then went to bed. He spent a much warmer and more comfortable night than the occupants of a battered Dormobile van that was parked on a stretch of flat stony desert some three hundred and fifty miles to the south-west.

The van was travel-stained and dusty, and had entered Afghanistan from Persia only twelve hours before. It was an old, second-hand vehicle, and some of the cheerfully daubed slogans were still readable under the blanket of dirt on the paintwork; slogans like, *The Three MustGetTheirs, Which Way Is East?* and *Kabul Or Bust.* The senior of this three-strong expedition was a heavy, red-faced man wearing a thick sheepskin coat. His features were those of an English farmer or market gardener, and he looked far from home. His two companions were of a type more usually found on a jaunt such as this, and were both wearing anoraks over sweaters and jeans. One was a younger man with a short, full beard, and the other a plain blonde girl with her hair drawn back and tied at the nape of her neck. Their passports described the party as a father travelling with his daughter and son-in-law, but in actual fact they were in no way related.

They had pitched a tent under the icily brilliant stars, but tonight the girl elected to clear a space for her sleeping bag in the back of the van. It was not through any false modesty, for normally she shared the tent with the two men. The reason was simply that tonight the van promised to be warmer. The interior of the Dormobile was littered with maps, clothing, foodstuffs, primus stoves, and all the necessities of a long trek and she had difficulty in making enough room to stretch her rather tall body. When she had settled herself her head was jammed close against a four-gallon water can that forced her to lay with a crook in her neck. She groaned audibly and sat up with the intention of dumping the can outside until dawn. Then she remembered that this particular can was the one with false bottom; the one that concealed the radio transmitter and the three Browning P-35 automatics. She swore gloomily and then lay down again, resigning herself to sleeping with a twisted neck.

Outside in the tent her two male companions suffered from the cold, and on the whole their sleep was disturbed as Simon Larren's might have been if he had known of their presence.

* * *

The following evening Larren was again in Caroline Brand's apartment. His day had been spent in making himself generally familiar with the streets and layout of Kabul, a routine procedure that could conceivably be an asset at a later date, even though he hoped to spend only a minimum amount of time in the city. Caroline had worked her regular daily hours at the library, but had also made a guarded telephone call to the local CIA man. While they waited for the American to arrive they drank more bourbon. It came from a bottle labelled *Old Kentucky*, and Larren was gradually beginning to enjoy the smooth, mellow taste.

Caroline said: "It was Ray who provided the bottle. He brought it with him on that first evening, but I think he regretted it afterwards. Anyway, even though he had to leave dissatisfied, he was too polite to take it back again."

Larren said cheerfully: "Here's to American politeness."

He drank, watching her, and wondering vaguely whether the American's dissatisfaction might have stemmed from something other than a mere lack of information and hard facts. Caroline was much colder than he remembered, and perhaps the American was the cause? Or perhaps he was the cause? Their old affair and its hopeless outcome might have affected her more than he realized. On San Quito she had been gay and wickedly alluring, and not all of it had been pretence. Now she was reserved, friendly but cool. He revised his first estimation and realized that she had changed, but the change was an inner one. She was older, or wiser, or sadder than she had been before. Or was that merely his imagination coupled with the long, prim and proper librarian's skirt? Or perhaps the transfer from the Caribbean sunshine to the bleakness of Afghanistan?

He was still speculating on the subject when they heard the sound of footsteps on the wide balcony outside. Knuckles rapped softly but clearly on the door, and Caroline lowered her glass and went to admit their visitor.

Ray Gastoni fitted the part that he had to play for his cover. He was big and solid, wearing a black donkey jacket with leather shoulders. His trousers were thick brown corduroy, picked for warmth and hard-wearing, and to complete the outfit he wore heavy-duty boots, and a black felt hat jammed on to his head. He was a construction engineer with one of the new American aid road projects, and he looked exactly like a tough gang boss. His face was a dark crag that betrayed the Italian parentage that had given him his name.

Caroline made the introductions, and when they shook hands Larren fully expected the American to try a palm-crushing grip. He was surprised when Gastoni refrained and for a brief moment they each tried to assess the other. Larren decided that Gastoni had probably been a road engineer before he had become a CIA man, but that was not unusual. The CIA made use of any amateur they could find.

Caroline filled up a third glass with *Old Kentucky*, tinkled in three large ice cubes, and tactfully ended the brief, appraising silence by saying:

"Here, I think I remember how you like it."

Gastoni nodded and accepted the glass, and then lowered his bulk into the nearest chair. He didn't drink and his eyes switched back to Larren's face again as he said:

"Okay, I'm listening. I know sweet damn all, so you can start from the beginning."

Larren pulled up another chair and sat down facing him. Caroline again preferred to half-sit on the edge of the table. Larren said:

"It's pretty straight-forward. I'm here to do a special job. It should only take a matter of days, but I'm going to need some local help. Not directly from you, I can keep you out of it. All I need is a reliable Afghani, and I'm hoping that you can loan me the right kind of man."

"And that's all!" Gastoni's tone was one of disgust and sheer disbelief. "That's all you'll tell me, and that's all you want!"

He stared for a moment, and Larren noted that he had black, shaggy eyebrows that joined in a straight line across the top of his nose. Then he laughed shortly, broke off his stare and with one casual intake disposed of two-thirds of the rye whisky in his glass. Without blinking he looked back at Larren, shifted forward in his chair and said forcefully:

"All right, I've stopped listening, and now it's your turn. For a start I don't like vague orders coming down from above without my knowing what's going on. I don't like the idea of you guys moving in on my pitch. I don't want to be compromised. Before you get any kind of help out of me I want to know a hell of a lot more about this special job — and even then I'm not making any promises. Does that get through to you?"

From the corner of his eye Larren saw Caroline make an eloquent shrugging movement of her shoulders. The words would have said, "I told you so," but Larren ignored her. He allowed Gastoni to finish and then said calmly:

"It gets through. My job is to make a trip over the Soviet border and bring out a man, one of our agents. On the face of it he defected to the Russians three years ago, but in actual fact he's still working for us and he's ready to come home. I'll disentangle him from the opposition myself, I only need your man to guide me in and out." That much Larren would have to explain to the guide who accompanied him, which meant that it would be relayed back to Gastoni anyway. He didn't see any need to elaborate and went on: "Apart from that I think the less we know about each other the better. That way we can't tread upon each other's toes."

The last sentence failed to have any mollifying effect. Gastoni was accustomed to having his own way, and no doubt he was quite capable of keeping an unruly working gang in order with his fists. He said flatly:

"Friend, I don't like the sound of these sheenanigins you intend to play around my doorstep. You're going to stir up a damn great hornet's nest and then skip out fast and leave me holding the baby. No, sir! This is one game that I don't want to play. You can go it alone if you're crazy enough, or else go back home. But you won't involve me."

Larren said softly: "Let's forget you said that, and then start again. You'll help me for the same reason that caused you to contact Miss Brand in the first place — the reason that causes you to be here now. And that is because you've had your orders from above."

Gastoni remained motionless, but behind his belligerency Larren could sense a shrewd brain ticking over. The American talked tough because that was the way he would normally get results, bullying his men into line. But he had to be smart enough to know when those methods would have no effect. The CIA would not employ him for his muscle alone, and that meant that despite the craggy exterior Ray Gastoni was nobody's fool. At last Gastoni said:

"That's a good point, Larren. And it makes me think that you're not levelling with me. Where's the American interest in all this? Why should my top-man order me to help you?"

"Good questions," Larren conceded. "But to the best of my knowledge there isn't an American interest. Your orders were the result of a straight trade between my boss and yours. I don't know the actual details, but my department came into possession of some information that was important to your people. One of our agents stumbled on to a leak from one of your embassies in the Middle East. We have mutual enemies, which makes us as anxious to plug leakages from your embassies as you would be to plug a leakage from one of ours. So the facts were passed on, and at the same time it seemed a good opportunity to request a little co-operation here in Kabul. That's why you received those orders to help me."

Gastoni said slowly: "That could figure, but there's one thing that you haven't reckoned on. My orders were only to contact Caroline, to find out what you guys were up to — and after that to use my own discretion. I haven't had a direct order to co-operate with you. And that means that I don't have to co-operate unless I think fit. My top-man wouldn't commit me blindly, no matter what kind of a deal he may have promised."

Larren had noticed the reference to Caroline, and not Miss Brand, and somehow that annoyed him. It may have meant nothing, and in fact he was almost sure it meant nothing, but the irritation was still there. The amount of dislike between himself and Gastoni was beginning to balance on either side, and he had to control his voice to maintain its calm level.

"Isn't it time we stopped antagonizing each other. All I want is to borrow a good Afghani agent for a few short days. There's no personal involvement for you, and I'm not trespassing into your field of operations. I don't even know what they are. If anything does go wrong then I'm the one who is going to get the chop. I won't even let your boy take any direct risks, at the first sign of trouble he can merge into the background."

Gastoni made a grimace, like someone contemplating a dose of medicine he knew he wouldn't like. Then he remembered the drink in his hand, finished it off and pushed himself up from his chair. He could have asked Caroline to fill the glass again, but he obviously wanted to think because he did the job himself. He didn't hurry, and stayed with his back to Larren as he tried the first taste. Then he turned slowly, pushing his left hand into the deep pocket of his donkey jacket. He said sourly:

"All right, Larren, I'll go along with you a little bit of the way. I'll do it because if I don't you'll probably hang around until your top-man has had another chat with mine and more orders start coming down the pipeline. They may be in my favour or in yours, but either way I don't want you hanging around all that length of time. Plus that there's the possibility that you'll try and go it alone, hire some local fool on your own account and then get your damn self killed. That way I could have trouble from two directions, from the reds and from my own side for withholding the right kind of help."

He paused and then finished: "I'll introduce you to a good man. In fact, the best available, because if you do get this crazy operation under way then I've no more desire than you to see it blow up in our faces. But you'll have to do your own asking, Larren, I'm not going to ask anyone to play suicide-chicken on your behalf. I'll put you in touch, but that is as far as I'll go."

"Well, at least it's a start."

Larren smiled, and allowed the smile to include Caroline Brand. He didn't need whole-hearted co-operation, just co-operation. Gastoni's heart was his own affair.

3

Through the Salang Pass

The man Gastoni had in mind was a young Afghani named Sardar Sharif, and although he rarely trusted first impressions Larren decided that Gastoni probably was keeping his promise to provide the best man available. Sharif was tall, an inch taller than Larren, with a dark, haughty face, sharp black eyes and a long, aquiline nose. His bearing was proud, a little arrogant, but was compensated by an easy smile and clean white teeth. At their first meeting he wore western clothes, a smart brown suit, white shirt and dark red tie. His English was excellent, apart from a slight mid-western twang, and Larren later learned that he had been college-educated in the United States. He came from an old and wealthy merchant family, well established in Kabul.

Gastoni brought him to Caroline Brand's apartment the following afternoon. Caroline was absent, stamping books in the British library, so only Larren was there to great them. The bottle of *Old Kentucky* had been finished the previous night, so without any preliminaries they went into the introductions and explanations. Sharif listened carefully to all that Larren had to say, and when asked for his help he smiled broadly and said:

"I think I would like to go along with you on this little trip. I am tired of sitting here in Kabul and doing nothing. And it will be one in the eye for those Goddamned Commies."

Gastoni was standing just behind Sharif's shoulder, and Larren saw the American's mouth tighten with annoyance. He knew then that Gastoni had been hoping that Sharif would refuse. That way the American would have been off the hook. There would have been no co-operation for Larren, but Gastoni wouldn't have been directly responsible for withholding it. However, the American's feelings were far from Larren's concern, it was the Afghani he needed.

Sharif's emphatic reference to "God-damned Commies" provided the clue to his character, and Larren guessed that he had been fully indoctrinated with the normal, panicky fear and hatred that America generated towards Communism. That would have happened during his years at college, which was undoubtedly where he had been suborned by the CIA, who would in turn have hammered the anti-Communist propaganda even deeper into his mind. If his father had chosen to send him to a Moscow university, then the process would have been reversed. He would have returned with a complete detestation of the West, and probably as an agent of the KGB. The latter reflection was beside the point, and now that he had the key to Sharif's support Larren turned it gently.

"As you say it will be one in the eye for the Commies. To snatch my friend out from under their very noses is going to make them look very silly. But even so, that's not the main aim. This friend of mine has been inside Russia for three years, and he's carrying a lot of information that will be invaluable to the West. If we can succeed in getting him out we'll have a clearer picture of what is going on inside Russia, and that in turn will help us to keep Communism in check." This was mere talk, for Larren had no idea of what kind of data Mannering was supposed to be bringing out, but it was impressing Sharif and so he kept an earnest expression on his face as he finished. "Everything is going to depend upon whether you can guide me across the frontier, and then bring the two of us back."

Sharif said definitely: "It can be done. But we shall need a vehicle of some kind to take us up to the Soviet border, and I take it that you have no transport."

He turned to Gastoni who had been glowering at Larren, but did not appear to notice the atmosphere between them.

"Ray, could you possibly loan us a Jeep or a Land Rover. Your construction company will not miss one for a few days. And we shall also need a reliable driver. The vehicle will have to be left in

Afghanistan while we cross the frontier, and to leave it unguarded — " Here he shrugged and smiled apologetically. "To leave it unguarded means that it will probably be stolen, dismantled and taken away piece by piece during our absence. There are many nomads in Afghanistan, and they are very poor people."

Gastoni was the only one standing, his feet apart and his hands plunged deep into the pockets of his donkey jacket. He tried to keep the scowl off his face as he considered, and at last he said doubtfully:

"I guess I can let you have a driver and a Land Rover. That's if you're determined to go along with this crazy limey?"

"But of course I am going." Sharif was smiling again. "Ray, I cannot understand why your people recruit me and pay me money, and yet so far have expected me to do nothing definite in return. It is so boring to sit at a desk and read invoices and make out orders for my father's firm. This is the kind of thing that I have been waiting for."

43

He turned back to Larren and continued eagerly:

"If Ray can get the vehicle and the driver, then I can be free to start tomorrow. Tell me now if you have any plans for making the actual crossing of the frontier?"

Larren did have some roughly formulated ideas, and they talked for the whole of that afternoon.

* * *

Despite Sharif's optimism the final planning and arrangements took another twenty-four hours, and it was the morning of the fourth day after Larren's arrival in Kabul when they started out on their mission. They left at dawn, when the first light of the sun was spreading like a stain of blood over the eastern barrier of the Hindu Kush. Darkness still clung to the narrower streets of Kabul, and in the wider streets there was only half light. The air was sharp and cold and Larren hoped that the sun would hurry its advance over the intervening mountains.

The Land Rover that Gastoni had provided was well used, but it had four-wheel drive and the engine was in first-class condition. With it came a grinning little man named Asefi, all bundled up in rags and a large turban who partnered the Land Rover the way Sabu had partnered his elephant. The two were inseperable. Larren was soon to find that Asefi had a quick sense of humour, together with the habit of chewing continuously on sticks of spearmint-flavoured chewing gum. He also smoked *Lucky Strike* cigarettes, and his English vocabulary was limited to a few choice words of American obscenity.

Nobody came to see them off. Gastoni had made it plain that he wanted no further contact with Larren whatsoever, and Caroline had decided that it was unnecessary for her to turn out at this unhospitable hour of the morning. The Land Rover had been standing ready overnight in a store-yard belonging to Gastoni construction company, with Asefi in attendance, and when Larren and Sharif arrived they were all ready to go.

Larren squeezed into the cab between the two Afghanis. Sharif had now discarded his smart western suit, and was wearing a turban and the shapeless combination of apparently second-hand clothing that distinguished most of his fellow-countrymen. All of them wore heavy overcoats and gloves. Asefi banged his hands together to warm them, started the engine and drove out of the yard. There was no traffic and very few people about as they circled the flank of the western of the two stony brown peaks that nipped Kabul at its narrow waist.

As they left the city behind the road turned due north, a smooth asphalt surface heading out between the mountain ranges of the Hindu Kush and the Kobi Baba. They passed a camping ground of nomads that was just stirring into life. Smoke still dribbled from the previous night's fires, and there were a few wild and shaggy camels tethered between the low black tents. It was a very poor camp, littered with heaps of refuse, a few collapsing handcarts, and some scratching chickens. Beyond the valley was mellowed by autumn. There were many spinneys of slender silver birch, some leaved in gold but mostly stripped bare by the keen winds. To the east the sun was softening its first blood-red advance, colouring the sky a more diluted pink. In the west the light was changing from grey to a soft pale blue, and the snows showed up like rich cream on the crests of the mountains. After an hour they no longer needed their heavy outer coats.

The four main cities of Afghanistan were positioned roughly on the four points of the compass. Kabul occupied the eastern point, to the south was Khandahar, to far west Herat, and to the north Mazar-i-Sharif. The only motorable roads linked these four cities in a crude circle, with the great, wild and mountainous mass of central Afghanistan almost untouched in the middle. The Land Rover was now following the east-north section of the road to Mazar-i-Sharif, the most adjacent point to the Soviet frontier, and from where a road continued north to Samarkand.

Asefi proved a capable and seemingly tireless driver, and during that afternoon they climbed the Salang Pass to cross the main range of the Hindu Kush that barred their way to the north. The landscape was wild and rugged, stark purple-red rock, valleys and rivers. They passed very little traffic, a few heavy lorries and once a lumbering bus. The lorries were all gay and colourful, for the Afghanis had a passion for decorating them with painted flowers and Disney cartoon characters like Mickey Mouse. Usually they were fully loaded with passengers, all clinging on in impossible positions, and the one bus appeared to be literally bursting with fierce bearded faces and turbanned heads popping from every window. The weather stayed fine the air was crisp and clear, but as they rose above the snow line the winds became colder. Then at eleven thousand feet the road entered the highest road tunnel in the world, thrusting for well over a mile through the heart of the mountain. The tunnel had been financed and engineered with Russian aid, and prompted Sharif to remark:

"All this Soviet aid would be a good thing if it were freely given. But it is not. There are hidden strings. Russia wants to extend her influence over Afghanistan, and if the Americans were not our friends I think they would find some excuse to march over us, just as the Chinese did with Tibet."

"And what of the American aid," Larren ventured quietly. "The fine new road from Kabul to Khandahar. Were there no strings there?"

Sharif turned to regard him with dark, level eyes. "You do not understand. The United States is ten thousand miles away, they have no territorial ambitions, and so their friendship is more genuine. There is no intention to dominate us." He smiled suddenly. "I can see the way your thoughts are moving, and I will admit that perhaps it is the American opposition to Communism that inspires most of their aid. And it is true that Afghanistan has to play both ends of the field, and accept aid from each side. We are a poor country and have to take what we can, and from where we can. But still we know which are our true friends, and which side has the better motives. Democracy is preferable to Communism, that is the basic truth. An Afghani is a fighting man, Mister Larren, and I have chosen my side."

Larren said: "I won't argue with you. I'm on the same side."

Sharif gave him the quizzical look again. "You sound cynical. Are you a cynic, Mister Larren?"

Larren reflected on that for a moment, and then nodded slowly.

"I suppose that perhaps I am. I didn't start out that way, but I've been doing this kind of job for too long, and most of the idealism wears off at the edges. In the end it becomes just another job."

Sharif said sincerely: "For Afghanistan it is not idealism, it is survival in the modern world. A slightly different outlook I think."

Larren conceded the point and the conversation flagged as they emerged from the tunnel. The road descended from the pass and the snowy mountains, dropping over five thousand feet into the far valleys where three turbulent rivers merged into one at the small town of Doshi. There they stopped in a crowded parking area beside the bazaar to stretch, eat, and purchase petrol. Larren was grateful for the break, but after an hour they continued on their way. The road now followed a wild gorge carved by the river that foamed past in a blue and white-flecked frenzy, and Larren was just a little bit dubious about the calm manner with which Asefi handled the Land Rover. The little man was an expert, but even experts could come to grief. However, Asefi chewed his sticks of gum, smoked his *Lucky Strikes*, and appeared to be quite happy as he casually manoeuvred the tricky bends and narrows that overhung the river.

Late in the afternoon they passed through the small townlet of Pul-i-Khumri, vaguely noted for its weaving and textiles, and here the road forked in two. The north road continued to the town of Kunduz, but the branching road to the north-west headed directly for Mazar-i-Sharif. Asefi hauled the Land

Rover round on to the new road and took the direct route.

They still followed the course of the river, crossing it several times before it swung away to their right. Larren felt stiff and cramped, and there were pins and needles prickling through his left leg. Dusk approached and the temperature began to drop, for there were sharp contrasts between day and night. Then at last they pulled into a small township named Haibak, and Sharif announced that here they would stop for the night. They had descended from the mountains into the great, arid basin of the sprawling Oxus River, still a hundred miles to the north, which formed the frontier line between Afghanistan and Russia, and the largest and most difficult part of the journey was behind them.

They stopped at one of the endless, hut-like tea or *chai* houses that served as resting-places for travellers and lorry drivers. Sharif bargained for blankets and a couple of mattresses in the corner where they could sleep, but Asefi chose to remain in the Land Rover huddled up beneath his overcoat. Larren shivered and pointed out that the weather was most certainly going to freeze during the night, but Sharif merely laughed.

"Have no concern for Asefi. This is a hard country, and we have a saying that if an Afghani lives to be seven years old then he will be immune from cold and disease and starvation. After that age only a bullet can kill him."

He clapped Larren on the back and finished: "Come, let us eat before we sleep. It will probably be rice and raisins again, similar to what we ate in Doshi. I am afraid that *chai* houses do not provide a very varied menu. But perhaps they will have spinach, and yoghourt made from goat's milk. You will like that?"

Larren shuddered, but he was hungry enough to eat anything.

★ ★ ★

The night passed without incident, and early the following morning they left Haibak and continued their journey. Sharif's boast about the spartan quality of the average Afghani appeared to be justified, for Asefi showed no ill effects from his uncomfortable night. He was as sprightly and as cheerful as before. The road was at first accompanied by a new river, but the snow-crested mountain ranges were now far behind them and eventually they were heading across stony plains, broken with ridges of bare rock, often in violent red and purple colours. Before noon they reached the small town of Tashkurghan, where there was another major cross-roads. Here they turned left on the road from Kunduz to Mazar-i-Sharif.

It was mid-day when they passed through Afghanistan's most northern city, but they did not stop and again turned directly north along the last fifty miles of road towards the Soviet frontier. They were now entering the wide belt of barren desert that ran beside the Oxus, and the landscape was turning gradually into empty sandhills. Sharif said quietly:

"At the end of this road is a bridge across the Oxus which leads into the Russian frontier town of Termez. From

Termez the road continues north to Samarkand where your friend Mannering is waiting to be rescued, but from here we have to take a more roundabout route to reach him."

Asefi was driving more slowly now, and Sharif was intently searching the horizon on all sides. Several times during the long drive they had glimpsed small encampments of nomads away from the road, and it was such a camp they needed now. It would be dangerous to take the Land Rover too close to the frontier, especially as they had to leave it behind for the next two or three days. For the last lap they needed some other kind of transport, and only the lawless nomads would be prepared to help them on a straight cash basis without too many questions asked.

Twice they saw low black tents close to the road ahead of them, but each time as they drew nearer they saw that the encampments were pitifully poor. The largest boasted only three tents and the smallest only one, and the occupants seemed to possess nothing but a few starving goats. Then, when they were a little less than twenty miles from the frontier, Sharif touched Larren's arm and said abruptly:

"Over there! On the horizon. A larger camp, and I think I can see horses."

Larren stared to their left, and it took him another half-minute to distinguish the huddle of distant tents that seemed to materialize slowly out of a shallow dip in the desert. He could pick out no details but Sharif had sharper eyes and continued cheerfully.

"If we are in luck we can hire those horses, and leave the Land Rover as a surety." He smiled and added: "With Asefi to make sure that they do not steal it and vanish."

Larren nodded, but said nothing, for suddenly he was beginning to have misgivings. The original planning had seemed sound, but there were no guarantees that they could trust these unknown wanderers of the desert, and careless talk relayed across the frontier could confront them with swift and unescapable disaster.

4

Across the Oxus

Asefi turned the Land Rover away from the road, bumping and lurching across the hard, barren sand until he pulled up a few yards short of the nomad camp. There were eight tents in all, most of them large enough to accommodate whole families. The tents were primitive, but by nomad standards the inhabitants were rich. They owned a score of goats, several camels, and four thoroughbred horses. No women were in evidence, but as they had approached Larren had noticed two dark, shrouded figures wriggling swiftly into one of the tents, and he guessed that the women were in hiding. Their menfolk were calm and unconcerned, some squatting, stilled in conversation, and some standing. They wore dark robes and large turbans, the latter usually with one loose end hanging down across the chest. The older men wore fierce, long beards, like biblical prophets, and all had alert, eagle faces. Those who had been squatting rose slowly to their feet, and Larren noted that they all possessed rifles.

Sharif said quietly: "Leave the talking to me. Stay in the Land Rover."

Larren nodded and watched as the Afghani climbed out on to the sand and then went forward to parley. The waiting men made no move, neither hostile nor friendly, but a nervous goat uttered a bleating noise to ease the silence. Sharif bowed slightly before the regal old greybeard who obviously ruled the group, and offered the first polite word of greeting.

It was a long conversation, which Larren would not have understood even if he had been close enough to hear the words. Sharif did almost all of the talking, with the old man nodding shrewdly and occasionally injecting a question. No one else interferred and the surrounding faces remained immobile. There was no way of telling what they were thinking, or how

Sharif's requests were being received. Larren could only watch and wait, and was vaguely conscious of a stiff ache in his back, for this had been another long, cramped day of driving. Beside him Asefi was relaxed, but watching with equal interest, and absently he unwrapped another wafer of spearmint chewing gum to add to the wad that was moving rhythmically around in his mouth.

Gradually the pattern of conversation changed, with the old man taking control and Sharif reduced to nodding and answering. Then there was a pause, during which the old man exchanged glances with the other elders who stood by him. One grizzled old veteran shrugged, two others nodded dubiously, and then the greybeard turned back to Sharif. Another string of words and it seemed that agreement was reached. Sharif smiled to include the whole party, and then came back to the Land Rover. He put his head inside and said:

"It is okay. They have agreed to help us in return for five hundred U.S. dollars.

The old man drives a hard bargain, but we expected that, and now that the bargain is made he will honour it."

"That's fine," Larren approved. "When do we start?"

"Tonight, as soon as it is dark. Until then we are the old man's guests, so please try to behave correctly." Sharif's grin became a little unholy as he advised: "Smile at everybody, and smack your lips when we sit down to eat. The meal will probably consist of some kind of goat's flesh stew, so if you are offered an eyeball, don't think about it — just swallow it quickly. You can pretend that it is an oyster. Oh — and a belch or two in the right places will be perfectly in order."

Larren winced, and was glad that he had included a tin of Entro-vyoform with his limited luggage.

★ ★ ★

When it came the meal was greasy but bearable, and eaten with their fingers. Larren kept up an unnatural smile with difficulty, making appropriate nods and gestures to the ragged circle of grinning brigands around him. The elders stayed polite and aloof, but the younger men viewed him with cheerful curiosity. They all ate with gusto, and with much kissing and licking of their fingers, and Larren did his best to keep pace. Mercifully no one pressed him into swallowing an eyeball, but he sensed that Sharif was enjoying a secret chuckle at his inner trepidation each time he was obliged to fish into the messy stew.

It was dusk when they finished the meal, and as the sun went down they began to prepare for the next stage of their journey. Larren stained his face, neck and hands until they were as dark as those of the Afghanis around him, and then he changed into a set of old clothes that Sharif had provided. There was a pair of baggy trousers of the kind peculiar to Moslems, a long khaki shirt which he wore with the tails flapping outside, and an old, much patched jacket which looked and smelled as though it had had at least half a dozen previous owners. To complete the outfit there was a little skull cap around which was wrapped a large turban.

Outwardly Larren was now Sharif's double, just another poor-class Afghani, but underneath his shirt was a money belt that contained one thousand roubles of Russian currency in used notes. The cash was for expenses and bribes if such became necessary. The belt also supported a waist holster cradling a Smith & Wesson .38 automatic, and strapped to his left forearm was a thin, sheathed knife. The rest of his equipment included a large jar of grease, and a pair of wire-cutters.

Three horses had been picked out, one each for Sharif and himself, and one for the guide who was to accompany them. There was little or no delay now that night had fallen, and the horses were swiftly saddled. They said their farewells to the old chieftain, saluted the camp in general, and then mounted up and rode off behind their guide. Asefi acknowledged their parting nod and lit himself another *Lucky Strike* as he watched them depart.

For two hours they cantered across the desert. The starlight showed them the rolling sand dunes, naked but for occasional dry, stunted bushes and patches of wiry grass. Sharif and the guide proved excellent horsemen, and fortunately Larren's training had been designed to prepare him for any eventuality. He knew how to ride a horse, even though the lack of recent practice indicated that he was going to be somewhat sore in places before the night was out.

They rode north-west, branching even farther away from the road, for they had no desire to strike the frontier too close to the official crossing point opposite Termez. The horses were sure-footed with high spirits, and even Larren's limited knowledge was enough to tell him that these were splendid racing animals. His own mount was a sleek black mare that would have been difficult to control if he had tried to do anything more ambitious than follow the fiery stallion that carried their guide.

It was midnight when they saw their first glimpse of the Oxus river, a deep, dark and looping barrier that cut across the desert. The greatest river in central Asia, it was one thousand five hundred miles from the Pamir mountains behind the Hindu Kush to the Aral Sea in central Russia. It created a formidable frontier line. Out in the plains of Turkestan it became sluggish and in places over three miles wide, but here it was fast although less than three hundred yards. They gazed at it for a moment, reining in their mounts on the crest of a sandhill, and then the guide spoke some kind of a warning to Sharif and the two Afghani turned their horses back into a sheltering hollow. Larren obeyed the silent signal from Sharif that indicated that he should join them.

They dismounted, a procedure which Larren followed stiffly and with some relief, and then Sharif said quietly:

"There are watchtowers on the far bank of the river, so we can go no farther on horseback. Our guide will take the horses back to the nomad camp, and from this point on we are on our own. On the third, fourth and fifth nights from now he will come back to this spot and wait for our return throughout the hours of darkness, with an extra horse for Mannering."

Larren said slowly:

"I don't doubt his ability to find this exact spot again and wait for us. But how the hell do we find him?"

Sharif's smile showed in the gloom.

"That is no problem. To our right, no less than half a mile from here, there is a tiny island, no more than a sandbank really, which divides the Oxus. That will be our landmark. We cross the river below the island, and provided that we arrive approximately in this area he will find us."

Larren had to accept that, and watched as Sharif conferred earnestly with their guide for a few moments. The man was nodding confidently, and finally he shook hands briefly with both of them, mounted his horse and with a wave began leading the two riderless mounts back across the desert. Larren watched him depart and then voiced his other fear.

"Can we really trust him to come back

for us? And can we trust his people to keep quiet?"

"He will come back," Sharif answered calmly, "They will rob and steal, and sometimes kill, but they will keep their word. And do not worry that they might betray us. These people are Moslems, and they do not approve of the way in which their religion is suppressed on the far side of the frontier. Communism, which does not believe in God, nor in personal freedom that is not controlled by the state, is an implacable doctrine which finds no friends among the nomads. The desert people will never accept Communism. This was one reason why they were willing to help us."

Again Larren had no choice but to trust in Sharif's calm assurance, but it was a little disconcerting to suddenly realize that he was now wholly dependent upon the young Afghani. He was in a situation where his own judgement was valueless and it was not a situation he could enjoy. He could only hope that Nevile Mannering would prove to be worth all the trouble that was being taken to get him out.

Sharif led the way and they climbed back up the slope of the sandhill. There was no immediate hurry and they conserved their energy as they crossed the last few hundred yards that brought them to the bank of the river.

Larren was assailed by more doubts. The river was much faster than he had previously visualized, a rushing black torrent that hissed and swirled with evil speed in the faint starlight. On the far side he could faintly distinguish low sand cliffs that would have to be climbed, and rising above them the dim silhouette of what might have been a wireless mast or a cable pylon. He remembered Sharif's warning and knew that this would be one of the watchtowers, spaced out along the frontier and manned by alert Soviet guards with powerful night glasses. Considering the more awesome barrier of the river they hardly seemed necessary.

The night was cold, and Larren shivered at the prospect of plunging into those freezing waters. However, Sharif was already stripping off his clothes, and it was too late to turn back now. Larren followed the Afghani's example, and they both stripped naked. The wind slid soft, icy fingers around their cringing limbs and Larren could feel his flesh goose-pimpling and turning blue with anticipation. Sharif looked at him and chuckled.

"Mister Larren, you look ridiculous. With black hands and face and a white body you will give the Russian guards a good laugh if they catch us."

Larren said shortly: "They're not going to catch us."

He hesitated to say more in case his teeth chattered, and began unscrewing the top of the large grease jar. It was the protective grease that long-distance swimmers used to combat the gnawing cold when they tackled such obstacles as the English Channel. He smeared it thickly over his body while Sharif secured their clothes in two separate bundles, each one wrapped in a light waterproof sheet. When he had finished.

Larren gave the half-empty jar to Sharif. The Afghani regarded it rather scornfully, but then condescended to give his own body a coating of the thick grease.

There was no conversation between them now. Their movements were swift and hurried, for the watchtower on the far bank was a danger that could not be ignored. They secured the two bundles on to their backs and began to descend the shelving bank of hard sand to the edge of the river. Here Sharif turned and held out his hand.

"Good luck. We may get separated, but don't worry. I'll find you on the other side."

Larren nodded and gripped the Afghani's offered hand. Sharif, he reflected, had a nice combination of native courtesy and civilized American politeness. Or perhaps he thought good luck and a handshake was still a British tradition.

They entered the river together. Larren didn't quite have the courage to dive forward, but the river tugged at his knees and hauled him in. The shock stopped his heart and lungs, and he floundered helplessly. The freezing black flood seemed to be pouring straight through him. He went under as his body was swirled away from the bank, and the current sucked him down into its watery grave. There was a roaring in his ears, as though the Devil himself was laughing hugely at his folly, and he was drowning in a rushing tomb of liquid ice. Down, down, down he went, down into the black gates of hell. And then, just when he was braced to hit the bottom, his head broke through the surface.

He gasped for air, and mercifully his paralysed lungs began to operate again. His heart began to beat, and his mind began to function. Only seconds ago he had not been able to tell the difference between going down and coming up, but now his brain began firing panic orders and he started desperately to swim. The current was sweeping him along at a fast pace, but he was lengthening the distance between himself and the bank he had left behind. He was not sucked under again and the panic began to subside. He had recovered from the first icy shock and now his blood was circulating once more. The current was dangerously cold, melted snows flooding down from the mountains, but he was a powerful swimmer and now that he had caught his breath he did not let it worry him. He did not fight directly against the current but allowed it to hurry him along. If he was washed half a mile downstream it was not wholly important. The important thing was to reach the other side.

He searched for Sharif, but there was no sign of another bobbing head caught up in the angry nightmare of the river around him. However, Sharif had been confident, and Larren was not unduly alarmed. They had expected to be separated.

He swam strongly with black waves breaking repeatedly into his face. The protective coating of grease and his own exertions helped to ward off the worst of the bitter cold, but he knew it would not last. He was well out into mid-river when it began to gnaw through to him again, and this time he knew that there could be no recovery as there had been from the first initial shock. Now he could not see either bank and his whole universe consisted of the black torrent of the river. He redoubled his efforts and could sense the first aching of his muscles which meant that he was tiring. Panic began to return.

He had been swept a long way downstream. The river was a living, taunting monster that jostled him along, and now his arms were becoming heavy. He saw the dark mass of the approaching bank, the sand cliffs rising above the black surface of broken water, and the panic sharpened into an acute stab of fear as he realized how swiftly the cliffs were moving past. He began to fight now, hurling the last of his energy into those final thirty yards to safety. The river seemed to tighten its grip around him, his arms and legs were a weary, leaden agony and the bundle strapped to his shoulders suddenly seemed to expand into a hostile mass that was striving to press him down. His chest was hurting now, a deep burning pain that threatened to stab down into his belly in a crippling attack of cramp. The icy river overwhelmed him and he sank below the surface, and then his knees struck gravel as he was tumbled along. New hope spurred through him and he made one last scrambling effort to get ashore. He felt gravel again beneath his clawing fingers and struggled to stand upright. The river swirled in cheated fury around his knees, and then he staggered forward and fell.

For several minutes he sprawled face down on a scrap of stony beach, his lungs sobbing painfully for breath. And then weakly he moved and crawled a little farther out of reach of the hungry river. A cold wind stung at his naked body and his teeth were chattering violently as he freed himself from the bundle on his back. He knelt beside it, tore open the waterproof sheet, and extracted the hip flask of brandy that he had brought especially for this occasion. He unscrewed the stopper and tipped the neat spirit down his throat, choking hotly, but feeling better as the brandy found its way into his stomach.

He was still shivering as he pulled

out a rough towel and quickly began rubbing himself dry, taking off the smeared coating of grease at the same time. If he delayed there was still a strong possibility that he would freeze to death, and so he rubbed himself vigorously before getting back into his clothes. Mercifully they had stayed dry, for he doubted if he could have survived the night in wet clothes. He checked that the vital Smith & Wesson .38 was still serviceable, and then took another long pull at the brandy flask. He felt fit now to wonder about Sharif.

He stood for several moments, staring both up and down the river. His eyes were accustomed to the starlit darkness and he could see that his miniature beach quickly ended, the river bank being broken up in each direction by sandstone rocks. There was no sign of movement, and the chill night wind took advantage of his lapsed defences to strike again at his heart. If the Afghani had drowned, then Larren knew that his own position was hopeless. He turned to look along the line of sand cliffs above and behind him, and then he received another shock. He was almost directly below the stark ominous outline of one of the frontier watchtowers.

5

Appointment in Samarkand

The watchtower could not possibly be the one that had been opposite him when he had started his swim, and Larren realized that he had been washed much farther downstream than he had first supposed. That fact worried him, but not half as much as the proximity of the tower itself. The high observation platform was deserted and there was no sign of movement behind the windows of the small wooden guard hut that it supported. However, there was a glimmer of light to indicate that at least one guard was in residence, and Larren hastily grabbed up the few traces of his arrival and moved into the dark shelter close below the overhang of the cliff. There was no snarl of machine guns, no flooding beams of light, and not even a cry to halt. The night was silent, and after a moment

Larren's heart began to beat more steadily as he crouched in the shadows. The guards manning the watchtower were probably sane, sensible Russians, cursing their boring duty with the firm conviction that no hostile agents would ever be suicidal enough to swim the Oxus. Like men on lonely guard duty anywhere they were probably dreaming of their sweethearts or playing cards.

Larren was breathing normally now, his shivers and his nerves were both under control. He had not been seen from the watchtower, but he still faced the nagging problem of finding Sharif. For the moment he refused to accept the possibility that the Afghani might have drowned, and forced his brain to reason on the assumption that they had both won through. Logically the stronger swimmer would land first, and his landing point would be above that of the weaker swimmer. The question resolved into which of them was the stronger swimmer? Sharif was hard as iron and would endure the rigours of the crossing more easily, but swimming was hardly likely to be a popular sport in Afghanistan and so he would be less adept. Larren finally decided that in this one respect he probably excelled Sharif, and so he chose to search downstream, below his own landing place.

He buried the sodden, greasy towel he had used to rub himself dry by simply ramming it down a narrow burrow bored by some local rodent in the sandy wall of the cliff. The other items that he had brought with him, the brandy flask, the rolled-up waterproof sheet, and the heavy wire-cutters, he distributed about the large pockets of his jacket. He had left no footprints along the stony beach, and having assured himself that no betraying signs were left behind he moved off in search of his lost companion.

Thin clouds had now shut out some of the brighter stars and for that he was grateful. He preferred the more stygian gloom. Darkness had always been his best friend and his natural home was the night. The only sound was the hiss and gurgle of the river as it flowed on its dark, eager course to irrigate the distant plains a thousand miles away. Sharif might be dead in its swollen, watery belly, but he would not think about that yet.

He scrambled silently over the rough, sandstone rocks, keeping as close as possible to the low cliff. He had no desire to move out into the open. He had travelled fifty yards when he heard a vague scratching sound behind him that triggered an instinctive warning in his brain. He moved into the blackest patch of shadow he could find and there was a primeval tingling in his blood. There was no silencer on the Smith & Wesson and so he ignored it. Instead his fingers stole inside the left sleeve of his jacket, freeing the knife strapped to his arm.

He saw a shadow loom out of the night, and felt a trickle of regret as he pushed the knife blade back into the sheath. A guard would have worn a fur cap, probably with ear flaps tied up, a heavy overcoat and boots, and at least a machine pistol in his hands. The man who approached him was tall, distinguished by a turban and a smiling flash of white teeth.

Sharif said softly:

"I calculated that the weaker swimmer would land further downstream, and so I came downstream to find you."

Larren smiled. There was no offence in Sharif's tone, just a plain statement of fact, and Larren chose not to mention that he had made exactly the same calculations. He said quietly:

"I'm glad you found me. There's still some brandy in the flask if you need something to warm your stomach?"

Sharif declined. "I thought you knew. I am a Moslem. I do not touch alcohol."

Larren apologized, and then they turned their attention to the task of climbing the cliff. They both knew what they had to accomplish and there was no more unnecessary conversation. The rushing sound of the river had drowned their first few words, but as they moved away from the river's edge it was just possible that the sound of their voices might filter up to the watchtower.

The cliff was not difficult to climb. They found a spot where a part of it had fallen away in a small landslide and were able to scramble up the steep slope of rocks and sand. They reached the top and their movements became slower and more cautious as the watchtower emerged once more into their line of vision. It was about fifty yards to their right, a gantry skeleton like the soaring steel neck of some giant baleful giraffe that guarded the next barrier to their progress, a high barbed-wire fence. The watchtowers were spaced at regular intervals along this part of the frontier line, but the next tower to their left was distant enough to be invisible in the night.

Larren crouched low on the edge of the cliff, and stared up once more at the high observation hut of the watchtower. There was still no sign of movement and he made a nodding signal to Sharif. The Afghani moved past him, silently and swiftly like a shadow in the gloom. He crossed the intervening stretch of open ground without wasting a second and dropped flat on his belly close beside the fence. There was no outcry from the tower. The night was still calm and peaceful. Larren drew a deep breath and then followed in a fast crouching run.

He threw himself flat beside Sharif and lay there panting. And then fear trampled abruptly over his heart as a sharp upright rectangle of white light showed high in the watchtower. A door had opened and the outline of a man came through it to stand on the encircling observation platform. Sharif swore, a soft, spitting sound that only Larren could hear, and they both pressed their faces flat against the dirt. Larren waited for the alarm, the click of the searchlight and the white, stabbing beam, but again it did not come. Larren tried to watch the distant guard, still keeping his nose in the dirt, and his eyes ached from trying to focus his vision from such an awkward angle. He saw the man come to the edge of the platform, his figure silhouetted by the light from the open doorway behind him. He was a heavy shape in a black greatcoat, the snub barrel of an automatic weapon snouting up over his shoulder. He paused on the platform edge and made a throwing movement into the darkness. Larren tensed, expecting an

82

exploding flare or a grenade, and then abruptly he realized how foolish a notion that was. The guard was simply throwing away some dregs of coffee or some other liquid from the two tin mugs he gripped in his hand. He turned and went back into his loftly eyrie, closing the door behind him.

As the rectangle of light vanished Larren began to breathe again. He relaxed and lifted his head, and beside him Sharif did the same. The Afghani smiled faintly with relief, but it was far from being a confident smile. They waited another minute for any fresh activity from the watchtower, and then turned to the fence.

Larren wriggled round until he and Sharif faced each other close by the fence where it was secured to a stout wooden post. He drew the wire cutters from his pocket and Sharif gripped the lowest of the taut strands of wire, holding it so that it could not recoil sharply, either to lacerate their faces or to make the high-pitched twanging sound that might alert the guards. Larren fitted the jaws of the cutters close to the post and neatly clipped through the wire. The faint click was audible but he doubted if it would carry up to the tower.

Sharif gently drew the wire away and then gripped the one above. Larren cut through two more strands and then they had a gap that enabled them to wriggle through. Sharif went first, squirming on his stomach, while Larren held up the wire above him, and then Larren followed.

Their final task was to restring the three cut strands of the wire so that the break was not immediately obvious. Larren carried some thinner lengths of wire in his jacket pocket, brought specially for the purpose of repairing the fence, and with these he rejoined the cut strands to the post. A close inspection would soon reveal that the wire had been breached, but Larren was hoping that the Russians were not in the habit of carrying out daily close inspections. With luck it might be months before the interference was spotted.

When the job was done they escaped

slowly into the night, keeping their stomachs and faces flat to the earth and wriggling forward like wary snakes. Larren had been well-trained for this kind of commando escapade during his wartime days with Special Operations Executive, and with many refresher courses since, and he was pleased to note that Sharif was equally proficient. When they had covered two hundred yards they felt confident enough to stand up and walked swiftly onwards across the desert. They had entered Soviet Russia, and now they had an appointment in Samarkand.

* * *

It was not long before they reached a road which they crossed quickly. The road paralleled the frontier and was not the one they wanted. A railway came next and they scrambled just as hurriedly over the tracks. Beyond was a mostly flat expanse of stony desert and they settled into a steady marching pace, moving in a north-easterly direction to their right, which they calculated would eventually bring them to the main north-bound road from Termez to Samarkand.

They took their guidance from the stars. Larren knew enough about desert navigation to plot a course, but he was an amateur beside Sharif. Despite his wealthy Kabul background the young Afghani had inherited all the skills and instincts of his nomadic forebears. He never faltered, and Larren soon gave up making cross-checks of his own as a waste of time.

They had several hours of darkness left, but they also had between five and ten miles of open country to cover before they reached the north road, and so they walked fast. From here they had to plan their movements as they came, their hopes for further progress were necessarily fluid, but they wanted to reach that road by dawn.

They were both feeling the cold after their freezing swim across the river, but gradually the exercise of walking warmed them. Their body-heat returned, and Larren decided that this forced march was as much a blessing as a curse. There was very little to see, just a general impression of hard barren sand. The terrain undulated slightly but never steepened into any real hills, although the horizon remained unseen. There was still enough cloud obscuring the heavens to make for an unusually dark night. Unusual that is for the desert where the skies would normally be brilliant and clear. Tonight the glory of the universe was masked, although the north star and a few others still showed to give them their bearings. From Larren's point of view it was a perfect night, and he could have asked for no better.

It took them five hours of non-stop walking to reach the road, and by then the dawn was clearing away the last shreds of shadow to reveal a cheerless landscape of dull red and brown. They had hurried their pace when the night had started to dissolve, and when they saw the road they were both breathing a little heavily from their exertions. Larren's thigh muscles ached, he was hungry, and he began to wonder whether he might not be getting just a little too old for these adventures. He was glad to see the dusty black ribbon of asphalt that was crossing their path from south to north. Far away to the north was a dark line of low mountains, and somewhere beyond was Samarkand. A romantic name, but experience had taught him not to expect too much from romantic names.

They searched along the roadside until they found a pile of red sandstone boulders where they could conceal themselves, and here they rolled one of the smaller boulders out into the middle of the road, just a little forward of their hiding place. Satisfied with their handiwork they returned to the main jumble of broken rocks and settled down to wait. Sharif produced some large slabs of chocolate and strips of dried meat from the pockets of his jacket and they ate a strange breakfast. It was a far cry from the bacon and eggs that Larren had allowed to inhabit his imagination during the last stage of their walk across the desert, but again he was too hungry to make any complaints. Afghanistan was not a country in which to be fastidious, and he was grateful for the American presence which had undoubtedly supplied the chocolate.

They were still eating when they heard the sound of an engine. A distant lorry was approaching fast from the direction of Termez in the south, and they quickly moved out of sight to watch developments. The lorry swirled up dust, roaring noisily, and then there was the sharp crash of hasty gear changes as the driver saw the large boulder that occupied a central position in the road. The lorry braked exactly opposite the spot where Larren and Sharif waited.

Two men got down from the cab, presumably they were Russian but they looked no different from their Afghani brethren on the south bank of the Oxus. Larren watched them and reflected on how ridiculous it was that political doctrine should divide peoples who were racially the same. They were grumbling, and just a little puzzled as to how the boulder came to bar their way. They glanced around uncertainly, and then bent over the boulder to roll it back to the side of the road. The back end of the canvas-hooded lorry was an open invitation, and Larren was startled when Sharif laid an abrupt hand on his shoulder to hold him back.

The Afghani shook his head warningly, and they continued to watch as the two men from the lorry succeeded in clearing the road and then climbed back into their cab. The engine started and the lorry pulled off, disappearing into another cloud of rising dust.

Sharif said calmly:

"I should have warned you that an ordinary truck is too dangerous for us. Transport is limited in this part of the world, and that driver will certainly stop and pick up any hitch-hikers he may pass. They will climb in the back and that would be disaster for us. We must wait for some kind of military or official vehicle which will pick up no passengers."

Larren was not over-happy with this new revelation, but he had to accept the basic reasoning and at this stage Sharif was the sole authority. He straightened his aching back and together they went to manhandle the big boulder back into the centre of the road.

They stopped two more heavy lorries, both coming from Termez, but each time Sharif shook his head and held back. The drivers clambered out cursing to clear the road and their third victim, a little shrimp of a man who had no companion to help him, almost exhausted himself with his grunting solo effort. Each time Larren and Sharif rolled the boulder back into the road to stop the next vehicle, and the third time they struck lucky. A massive army lorry rumbled to a stop with a snarling of brakes.

The cab door opened and a man dropped cautiously into the road. He was a White Russian wearing a dusty uniform with the rank tabs of a Lieutenant in the Soviet Army. He wore a fur cap but no greatcoat, and his fingers hesitated over the smooth leather flap of the holster that contained a revolver at his hip. He was doubtful that the boulder could have barred his way of its own accord, and yet he obviously thought it fanciful that it should have been moved there deliberately. Indecision played across his face, and for a moment Larren feared that he meant to investigate the pile of rocks where he and Sharif were hiding. Then the Lieutenant decided not to risk making a fool of himself in front of a subordinate and shouted to his driver to get down and clear the road.

The soldier at the wheel obeyed promptly, gripping the offending boulder with both hands and pushing hard. He coughed audibly, and after a moment the Lieutenant went to help him. No heads had popped out of the back of the lorry to enquire what was happening, and the very fact that the young officer had not called for further help indicated that the lorry had no more passengers. Sharif glanced at Larren and nodded.

They moved together, keeping low behind the screen of rocks and dodging swiftly and silently to the back of the lorry. The Lieutenant and his driver were still busy at the front and Sharif quickly unfastened the canvas tail flaps. Larren reached for his knife but it was not needed. The Afghani's strong fingers tore apart the restraining cords, and then he was up and into the back of the lorry, using Larren's braced shoulder as a stepping stone in one lithe vaulting movement. He turned and reached out a hand, Larren caught it and followed almost as swiftly.

They closed the flaps and froze. They could still hear the grunts of the driver and the panting curses from his officer, and exchanging smiles they relaxed. Sharif refastened the opening in the canvas and Larren briefly examined the large, hooded interior of the lorry. It contained a score of waist-high petrol drums, and when he tested one for weight he found they were empty. Sharif came to stand beside him and they listened in silence for sounds from the front.

They heard the two men getting back into the cab, both breathing heavily, and the Lieutenant made some angry remark which Larren could only guess at, but which brought a broad smile from Sharif. The engine had been left running and now it roared more noisily as the driver shifted into gear and accelerated away.

Sharif said softly:

"There is no army encampment between here and Samarkand, and no towns of any mentionable size, so I think it reasonable to hope that we shall get a free ride all the way. However, there may be police or military checkpoints, so it will be best if we can be well hidden if anyone glances inside. A thorough check is unlikely with a military vehicle, but we must be prepared for routine."

Larren nodded, and together they began the necessary re-arrangement of the lorry's cargo. There was plenty of engine noise to drown any sounds they might make, and soon they were settled as comfortably as could be expected in a small space behind the drums they had shifted forward. Outside the dry hills and plains were speeding past and they were approaching the northern ranges that had to be crossed before they reached their final destination. Until then they could only relax, and endure the heavy rattling movement of the lorry, the smell of petrol and the taste of the dust that was flung up by the wheels to filter through the floorboards. Relax and endure, hope and wait. They were playing the game by ear, and luck had a good deal to say in calling the tune.

6

The Strike

Some benevolent fate, or patron saint of needy cloak and dagger agents, must have directed their choice of transport, for after a long day of cramped and uncomfortable travelling they eventually arrived in Samarkand. There had been two checkpoints soon after they had started their journey, but in each case the precautions they had taken to hide themselves were sufficient. They lay silent and unmoving when the lorry stopped, listening to the exchange of words between the two men in the cab and the soldiers or police guards who had ordered them to halt. Sharif later explained that the Army Lieutenant had been obliged to state his destination and his business on each occasion. The only inspection was limited to a brief glance into the back of the lorry, although on the second occasion they did begin to sweat when a man climbed aboard and checked that the petrol drums were empty as stated. Sharif carried a folded road map inside his coat, and when the lorry was on the move again he marked in the approximate positions of the two checkpoints. The information had to be remembered for the return journey.

After the first two hours the road began to climb and they knew they were entering the range of mountains they had been able to see at the start of their journey. The road cut through the lower, western heights and here there was another stop. Larren and Sharif exchanged glances and tensed themselves in anticipation of another prying head peering into the back of the lorry. However, nothing happened. Sharif listened to the sound of voices on the far side of the canvas hood and then relaxed. He explained that they had paused in a small town where the Licutenant and his driver had obviously decided to rest and eat.

Their unknowing benefactors were in no hurry, for it was another hour before they came back to the cab and the lorry lurched forward again. Larren and Sharif had been obliged to keep quiet and keep low, and they were glad to be able to stand upright and stretch when the lorry resumed its northward progress. Occasionally they glanced out through the back of the lorry at a landscape of violent and mostly barren hills, but they were careful not to move about too much in case they were caught away from their hiding place by an unexpected halt. There was no need for them to worry unduly about their exact location, for their map showed only two possible side turnings in two hundred miles. Both were very minor roads, and in any case Sharif was certain from the conversation overheard at the two checkpoints that the lorry was bound for the same destination as themselves.

There were two more long stops at intervals during the day, and each time the Lieutenant and his driver dismounted to relax in one of the roadside *chai* houses. Larren longed to do likewise, but during the halts he and Sharif had to remain very still, denied any movement or conversation. The Afghani did not seem unduly bothered, but Larren was beginning to feel that *rigor mortis* was taking creeping control of his muscles. The floor-boards of the lorry were apparently made of the world's hardest oak, and he was beginning to be plagued by thirst.

It was late in the afternoon when they reached Samarkand. The lorry slowed its pace to enter the city, and the bustle of movement and the sounds of other traffic around them told them that they had arrived. They heard the clank of what could only be a tram rattling past, and they both knew that Samarkand was the only city in this remote area of Russia that was large to boast of trams.

They both moved stiffly to climb over the petrol drums that shielded them from the back end of the lorry, and risked drawing open the canvas flaps by a few inches so that they could see out. They were entering an obviously growing modern city and another tram went rumbling past on shining steel lines. To their left they were passing a large, tree-shaded park and to their right modern but unimaginative blocks of shops. The people thronging the wide pavements were reminiscent of Kabul, a scattering of smart western styled suits mixed up with shabbier men wearing large turbans. The difference was that here there were women in western clothes as well. Larren observed, and was glad that he had not allowed himself to be misled by the glamorous name of Samarkand, although he guessed that the old city, the capital of Tamerlane's Mongol Empire and the crossroads of the ancient silk road to China, would still exist beside its new counterpart.

However, this was not the time to ponder on the glories of Samarkand's past. Their present transport had served them well, far better than they had any right to expect, but now their most pressing problem lay in how to get out unseen and merge into the streets. They had no desire to be carried beyond the city, or to wind up in an army camp, and so there was no time to lose.

Mercifully it was getting dusk, but even so their escape became a risky proposition. Twice their lorry was halted by the traffic at busy junctions, but each time other vehicles drew up close behind so that they could not jump out unseen. Then came a third stop and for a moment the road behind them was clear. There were a few people passing on the nearest pavement, but there was no sign of a policeman. They had to take a chance and this looked like being the best they would get. Sharif pushed open the canvas flaps and jumped down into the street, brushing himself down calmly as though he were a legitimate passenger who had every right to be quitting the vehicle at this stage. Larren dropped down beside him and then turned back to lace up the flaps, another natural gesture by a *bona fide* traveller. The lorry moved off and they walked away from behind it, stepping on to the pavement and walking back the way they had come. There was a large shop window beside them that reflected their disappearing lorry, and Larren's heart took a sudden tumble as he saw that there had been a policeman directing traffic at the road junction behind them. However, there was no curt command to stop and explain themselves and they eased into the now thickening crowd.

They kept walking and Larren was disturbed to note that a great many of the faces that passed them were distinctly Mongoloid in appearance. There were a great variety of other facial characteristics, but even so he and Sharif were not blending as unnoticeably into the background as he would have liked, despite their shabby clothes and turbans.

It was now that Larren became one-hundred-per-cent dependent upon Sharif. The language here, apart from the official Russian, was a related dialect to Turkestan, and he knew only a little of the former and none of the latter. Sharif understood the local tongue as well as the pushtu tongue of Afghanistan and only he could communicate. Larren was reduced to playing a dumb role and hoping to get away with it for a brief period of time needed to snatch Mannering and make a lightning retreat.

Twice Sharif stopped and asked his way, and eventually they left the growing new city with its wide, treelined streets and naked concrete blocks behind. They entered the older parts of Samarkand where there were crumbling remnants of Persian and Islamic architecture. They crossed a wide square where the three famous Moslem colleges had once been the home of Arab culture, but now it was dark and they were in too much of a hurry to absorb details. Sharif asked his way again and then turned up a narrow street in the poorest part of the old city. He paused before a dingy cafe, explained that it was also a cheap lodging house, and then led the way inside.

The place smelled, it had a low roof of sagging beams and plaster and was lit by the smoky glow from a few strategically placed paraffin lamps. A group of men in turbans and shapeless clothes glanced up and stared from a corner where they had been gambling with grubby cards. An old man with a yellowed Mongol face came a pace forward and stared even more enquiringly, and Sharif began to speak to him. Larren stood back patiently and tried to prevent his nose from curling with disgust. The smell was a combination of trapped smoke, greasy food and human sweat. He thought that he could detect hashish as well but he was not sure.

The haggling did not take long, and after a few minutes the old man turned away and started to climb a wooden staircase that led to the rooms above. Sharif made a silent signal to Larren and the two men followed him. Curious eyes watched them depart, and then a man spat on the floor and called attention back to the game of cards.

Larren and Sharif were shown into a cramped, box-like room where they both had to duck their heads to enter. There was no light except the starlight that came through an open window, but Larren could distinguish two straw mattresses laying on the floor. There was another short conversation between Sharif and the old proprietor, and then money exchanged hands and they were left alone. They could hear the old

Mongol wheezing heavily as he descended the stairs, and then Sharif said very softly:

"I think he is satisfied that we are genuine travellers from the south. Fortunately the Soviet Union is a vast country with a variety of different dialects in the more remote parts, so I have been able to explain your silence and lack of understanding. I have also told him that you are sick and will probably be confined to your room for the next twenty-four hours. I am sorry, but I think that is the best way. You will stay in hiding while I locate the precise address of this hospital where your friend is being treated."

Larren said ruefully: "Thank God I've got an open window, otherwise I don't think I could stand it. But can you be sure that the old man won't report us to the police?"

"I don't think that will happen. If he can keep his guests quiet he can avoid paying some of his taxes. In places like this they are not as strictly law-abiding as they should be. A proper hotel would report us immediately as a matter of routine, but here we should be safe. In any case, like jumping out of the lorry, this is a chance that we have to take. This job is full of risks, and we must have somewhere for you to stay out of sight while I reconnoitre."

Larren nodded, and had to accept that Sharif was right.

★ ★ ★

They were able to order a greasy meal, a vague stew with some kind of unidentifiable meat and flat loaves of unleavened bread which was brought to their room. They slept uneasily through the night and at dawn Sharif left on his mission. Larren remained imprisoned in their cubicle of a room with no other task except to get back under his single ancient blanket and make sick groaning noises if he should chance to hear footsteps approaching the door. Ironically he did have an unpleasant pain in his stomach, and throughout the morning he feared that the previous night's supper had favoured him with an attack of dysentery.

That was the last thing he wanted, and he was relieved in the afternoon when the discomfort disappeared without having any undue effect upon his bowels. He was hungry again but he played safe and ate the last of the chocolate that Sharif had left behind.

It was a long day, but although there were plenty of voices sounding from below and occasional footsteps shuffling past his door no one came to disturb him. The single window was set high and showed him nothing but a square patch of blue sky. Street noises filtered upwards, and he had nothing to do except listen, and quell the troubled thought of how he would act if Sharif failed to return. He had plenty of past experience in the art of seemingly endless waiting, but he had never been wholly patient with delay and this time it seemed harder than usual. The day darkened into dusk again before he heard a definite footstep outside the door, and quickly he regained his mattress and drew up his blanket.

Sharif must have heard the faint scuffling sound, for he was grinning broadly when he opened the door. He looked tired, and in one hand he carried two more plates of the repulsive stew. He talked cheerfully in the local dialect as he closed the door with his foot, and then he lowered his voice and said in English:

"I hope you have an appetite. I have brought some more food."

Larren shuddered but accepted one of the plates. There was no more chocolate and so it was a simple choice of risking dysentery or starve. Sharif squatted beside him and began to eat hungrily, and Larren gave the Afghani time to finish his meal before he asked:

"Well, how did you enjoy your tour of Samarkand?"

"Samarkand is a very interesting city. Did you know that it contains the tomb of Tamerlane?" Sharif smiled as he spoke, soaking up a last patch of grease with his last piece of bread and popping it into his mouth. He put his plate down and then continued. "But I don't suppose you have any interest in the bomb of Tamerlane. I had to go back to the modern part of the city to find out what we need to know. There is a general hospital here, but they would be unlikely to treat your friend. The most likely place is the Lenin Institute. That is a large new nursing home which caters especially for nervous disorders, a kind of psychiatric hospital. The patients are all sent down from northern cities for treatment which includes a long convalescence, and I think they are all important people, scientists, technicians, and high party officials. There are no bus drivers or ordinary workers at the Lenin Institute."

"It sounds as though it must be the place. Are you sure it's the only one of its kind?"

Sharif nodded. "It is the only private mental hospital in Samarkand. Today I must have walked a score of miles in exploring the city and asking questions. Of course, I had to ask my questions carefully, I could not make direct enquiries, but I am sure as it is possible to be in the circumstances. If your friend is being treated for a mental breakdown here in Samarkand then he must be at the Lenin Institute. There is nowhere else."

Larren was satisfied that Sharif would have done his job thoroughly, and pushed away the last of his doubts. He became more practical and said:

"Have you seen the Institute? Can you give me details of its location and defences?"

Sharif nodded. "I have been there. It is on the out-skirts of the modern city, a very big building with lawns and grounds where the inmates can take exercise. There is a police guard at the gates, and the whole area is surrounded by a ten-foot wall. However, I think that we should be able to get over the wall easily enough."

Larren shook his head. "Sorry, Sharif. This next stage is my turn to go solo. I'm going over that wall alone."

The Afghani stared, and then laughed.

"How can you? You will need me to find out which room contains your friend!"

Larren smiled. "That's a good point, but I've already worked out the answer.

I'll make for the reception desk and examine their records. It's a private hospital, so although there'll be night nurses on duty I don't expect to find anyone on reception. I can read enough Russian to recognize Mannering's name, so I should be quite capable of managing alone. You'll stay outside for two reasons. One is that I want you to hire a taxi so that you can pick me up at midnight a couple of blocks away from the Institute. With luck I should have Mannering with me. The second reason is that I promised Gastoni that I would do this bit alone. If I don't make that rendezvous on time then you'll have to look out for yourself and make your own way back to Afghanistan."

Sharif argued, but this time it was he who had to accept the facts and finally they agreed.

★ ★ ★

It was an hour before midnight when Larren and Sharif parted company within sight of the Institute. Apart from one short ride on a clanking tram they had walked from their lodging house in the old city, and although the darkened streets were sparsely populated at this time of night they had not been challenged. Now Larren was feeling fit and confident, partly because of their successful run this far, and partly because he had escaped from the claustrophobic hovel that had been their room. Whatever happened they were not going back.

Sharif departed on his search for a taxi and Larren approached the high walls of the Institute alone. He dared not risk being challenged now and speed was essential. This was a quiet area, chosen for its solitude, and the street was deserted. Street lamps threw pools of light at intervals from tall concrete posts, and farther along the wall Larren could see another splash of light that marked the main gateway. A lone policeman stood on duty, muffled against the cold in a fur cap and a heavy black greatcoat. He wore a black leather belt and revolver holster outside the coat, but for the moment his back was towards Larren. The corner of the wall was lit by another street lamp and Larren felt his heart quicken as he hurried across the illuminated patch of the road. The policeman did not look round and Larren took cover behind the corner of the wall. He had not been seen and so he turned away, following the line of the wall away from the main road.

About halfway along the wall he stopped in a patch of black shadow. He tensed and then jumped. His hands caught the top of the wall and he heaved himself up. He didn't hesitate on the top but simply rolled his body over in a continuation of the original movement and dropped on the far side. He landed in a patch of shrubbery that made an alarming amount of noise and instantly crouched down. No one came to investigate and then he began to breathe again.

He could see the main building now, through a curtain of trees and across neat lawns. The palms of his hands were sweating a little and he wiped them dry down the thighs of his baggy trousers. Then he reached underneath his shirt and drew out the Smith & Wesson .38. He didn't intend to use it, for the sound of a shot would be fatal, but it would be very effective for threatening anyone he might encounter into silence. If he was forced to kill he would use the knife.

He moved towards the darkened hospital, taking the route that offered the most cover. Even beyond the trees there was plenty of shrubbery breaking up the lawns, and although every sense was alert he felt supremely confident. He had done this sort of thing before and he always enjoyed it. Stealth and silence were part of his nature, sharpened by experience and training.

He circled round to the front of the building. The main entrance was unlit and he made no sound as he went up the broad white steps to the closed doors. Through the glass he could see that there were no lights in the corridors beyond the reception hall, but the hall itself was in darkness. He tried the door and found that his patron saint was still smiling benevolently over his shoulder. The door was not locked. However, with a police guard at the main gates that was probably considered unnecessary. His greatest asset was the fact that no one at the Institute really expected intruders.

He closed the door behind him and crossed to the reception desk. He laid the Smith & Wesson down upon a clean white blotter and then took out the slim pencil torch that was part of his standard equipment. He narrowed the hooded beam until there was a minimum of light, and then carefully searched through the contents of the desk. There were neat little piles of official cards and forms, but in the left-hand drawer he found what he wanted, a row of files in alphabetical order, each one recording details and brief case-histories of each of the hospital's inmates. There were three files under the letter M. The first one was Mannering's and the pinprick of torchlight quickly settled on the only details he wanted. Mannering was in room number 25 on the second floor.

Larren smiled briefly. His one fear had been that Mannering might have been removed from the hospital before he arrived, but now that the man was in his grasp he felt that his mission was almost complete. Unless Sharif ran into trouble all three of them should be heading south into Afghanistan within the hour. His patron saint was working overtime tonight and he had hopes of being back across the frontier before dawn.

7

The Fast Return

He tidied the reception desk as neatly as he had found it, closing all the drawers. Then he switched off the needle beam of the torch and returned it to his pocket. He picked up his automatic and listened, but the interior of the large building was still and silent. A corridor led inwards, and there was a light at the far end to show a broad flight of steps leading upwards. Larren moved towards the light, circling the desk and avoiding the large bust of Lenin that occupied a centrally placed pedestal in the hallway. He spared a thought to wonder if there were any new buildings in the Soviet Union that were not named after Vladimir Ilyich Lenin.

The corridor became brighter as he moved towards the stairs, but there was no sound from behind the many doorways leading off on either side. Larren reached the end of the corridor, glanced around the corner, and saw another large desk where a night duty nurse in a crisp white uniform sat writing, He had to cross three open yards to reach the staircase, but the nurse only needed to glance up to see him.

Larren wondered whether he should retreat and attempt a new line of approach, but before he could decide the nurse made a testy sound of annoyance, sorted over the forms on her desk, and then got up and walked directly towards him. Larren took a step back down the corridor, his free hand encountered the nearest door-knob and he turned it quietly. He backed into a pitch black room only seconds before the nurse turned the corner. He heard her steps as she went past, listened harder and heard the faint sounds of breathing from somewhere behind him.

He had no wish to startle some neurotic patient from a shallow sleep, and so just as silently he re-opened the door and returned to the corridor. The nurse had now reached the reception hall and her back was towards him as she switched on the light. He saw her move to the desk and guessed that she had run short of one of the many varieties of forms that were kept in the drawers. His nerves jittered with the thought that he had only just avoided a head-on collision, but he was too experienced to let the jittery feeling last for more than a second. He still had the blessing of fate, or luck, or whatever agency was guiding his footsteps, and so he grabbed his opportunity to run over to the staircase.

Half a minute later he was on the second floor. His eyes and ears were alert to detect the first approach of another patrolling night nurse, but there was nothing to alarm him. The corridors were brightly lit but deserted. A helpful sign indicated rooms 20 to 28, and it took less than another half-minute to locate number 25.

Again he smiled, it was all too easy, but then abruptly the smile faltered on his face. There was a line of light showing from underneath the door of number 25, and that was something that he had not expected. It did not necessarily mean any more than that Mannering was awake, perhaps reading or unable to sleep, but Larren had a vague premonition that his patron saint had chosen to desert him. He pressed close to the door but heard nothing. There was an eye-level inspection panel that was closed, but after a moment's hesitation he eased the sliding panel gently to one side.

He opened it a bare inch, just enough to see the interior of the room with one eye. It was a pleasant, but not over-luxurious private ward. At the moment it was occupied by two men, one dressed in blue pyjamas on the bed, the other wearing a dark suit sat with his back towards Larren in a bedside chair. Neither moved or spoke, and the man on the bed had an expression of thoughtful concentration, his hands were resting on his knees. Larren was puzzled, and then he realised that there was a small table and a chess board between the two men.

Larren cursed inwardly. The man in the blue pyjamas was undoubtedly Nevile

Mannering. The fat, unimpressive English face that looked as though it had been moulded out of suet pudding was the same one that had gazed out of the front pages of every British newspaper during the 'vanished diplomat' sensation three years ago. There were more lines etched across the temples, the grey hair was thinner with patches of white, but it was the same man. Larren felt the build-up of frustration and wondered why Mannering had to choose tonight of all nights to sit up late and play chess.

As he watched Mannering's partner made a move, leaning forward to shift his piece and then straightening up. Larren caught a glimpse of a dark, cruel face, and felt a repeat performance from the wriggle of unease that had affected him when he had first realized that Mannering had company. There was something strangely familiar about that face too, but he could not place it. The problem lingered for a moment in his mind, but then he pushed it aside. The immediate problem lay in deciding his next move. He couldn't approach Mannering until the second chess player had gone, and so he had to find somewhere to wait unseen.

He mover farther along the corridor, dubiously studying the choice of doors. At the far end he found a toilet and bathroom and went inside. He left the door ajar so that he could see into the corridor and waited.

Twice he had to close the door as a night duty nurse went past on her rounds, but fortunately no one came to use the bathroom. Then after half an hour there was a movement from number 25 and he saw the man in the dark suit emerge. He bade Mannering good night, and then added in English:

"I will leave the problem with you until morning. If you can save your bishop without losing your knight I shall be very interested to see how it is done."

Larren watched the man depart, and little notes of warning were pinging along the radar screen of his nervous system. The man in the dark suit did not look like a doctor, and his confident behaviour made him look even less like a patient. There was something wrong somewhere and Larren sensed trouble in the stranger's presence.

When the corridor was clear Larren remained still for a moment, thinking hard, but then he realized that by now Sharif should be waiting for him with a taxi and it was dangerous to waste any more time. Again his thoughts had to be set aside while he tackled the job in hand. He left the bathroom and hurried back to number 25.

Mannering was still sitting on the bed, his head bowed as he studied the chess board. He did not look up immediately when the door opened, perhaps thinking that his chess partner had returned, and Larren was able to close the door before the other realized that anything was amiss. Then Mannering looked up and his face turned white, his body jerked as though he had been stabbed in the back.

"What on earth — I mean who — "

His voice faltered weakly and collapsed, and Larren had to remember that at the moment he was dressed like some wild Afghani thug, and that there was a gun gripped in his hand. He lowered the Smith & Wesson, tried the nearest he could get to a reassuring smile and said softly:

"Easy now. I'm a friend. I may not look much like it, but I've come from London. Smith gave orders to get you out."

Mannering stared at him. "You're crazy! You're off your rocker. I can't get out of here. Not now. It's impossible now."

Larren realized that Mannering was bady frightened. It was something he should have been prepared for. The very fact that the man was in a mental hospital should have been obvious, and yet Larren had assumed that Mannering had been feigning a breakdown in order to get this close to the frontier. He tried to make his voice sound more friendly and said:

"You asked Smith to get you out, remember? That's why I'm here."

"That was over three months ago. Things have changed since then. When I knew I was being sent down here for a rest I thought there was a chance to escape, but not now."

Larren was annoyed, but tried to hide the fact.

"Why not *now*? What's changed?"

Mannering passed his tongue over his lips, they were weak, fleshy lips. The man had gone to pieces badly and it was a moment before he could reply.

"You must have seen the man who just left my room. The man who was playing chess with me before you came in. Didn't you recognize him?"

Again the tremor down Larren's spine, but he shook his head.

"No, who was he?"

Mannering took a deep breath. "His name is Korovin. Whitehall has a file on him that's two inches thick. Surely the name must mean something to you?"

The name did mean something. Larren's mind went back to a dimly remembered file, one of the many devoted to known hostile agents that was kept in the big steel file behind Smith's desk. He compared the dark, cruel face he had only half seen with the memory of a poor photograph clipped to the file, and he knew why the face had seemed just vaguely familiar. The full name was Vaslav Semyonovich Korovin, one of the most efficient operators of the KGB, with a reputation as a killer that was unmatched even in that highly ruthless organization. Larren understood now why Mannering was afraid, and why his own senses had been disturbed. He had subconsciously recognized one of his own kind, and he knew that his stars were no longer in the ascendant. He said slowly:

"I know a little about Korovin. But what the devil is he doing here?"

"Isn't it obvious? Korovin is here to watch me. They know that I'm expecting someone. How they found out God only knows. I thought that the contact I used to reach Smith was perfectly safe. But somehow they know or suspect that I'm waiting for something like this to happen. That's why I can't leave with you. You'll have to get out now, as fast as you can." Mannering's face was urgent and showing a sheen of sweat. "You're a dead man if you stay here. You must leave."

Larren's mouth tightened, and he knew that he had real trouble on his hands. Mannering was a beaten man, a mental and physical wreck, he was terrified for his own skin, and yet somewhere in that tormented mind there were facts and figures that Smith needed. At this stage it was adding lunacy to lunacy to consider leaving empty handed. Whether Mannering liked it or not his rescue was going through as planned. Larren sharpened his voice and said:

"Get a hold on your nerves. You can't afford to crack up completely. I'm leaving, but you're leaving with me. I didn't come all this way just to hear that you've had another change of heart." Mannering was staring at him again but he went on brusquely. "Does Korovin, or anyone else, check up on you during the night?"

"No, but — "

"Well that's fine. That means that we have between six and seven hours' start before you'll be missed. By the time the alarm is raised in the morning we should be safely over the frontier."

"You might be. I'm not coming!"

Mannering had straightened up from the bed and was putting on a brave face. It crumbled when Larren raised the Smith & Wesson and told him bluntly:

"You have no choice. If necessary I'll crack this across your head and carry you out. And remember, if I fail, or if you give the alarm, then we are both in the same mess. At the moment the KGB can only suspect that you got a message out and that you're planning another double-cross, but once my presence becomes known they'll be sure. They'll have no mercy on you then. Your chances of survival are linked with mine. Even if you do stay behind, you're still finished if I get caught. You yelled, for help, and now you've got it. You have to co-operate!"

Mannering was trapped and he knew it. Fear and dejection struggled on his pasty face, and then he said helplessly:

"But how? How can we escape?"

"Don't worry about it. Just get dressed and leave everything to me. We've already wasted too much time in arguing, and if the night nurse should happen to walk past and overhears us then we're finished."

Mannering hesitated, biting his lip, and then he turned to the tall locker that stood beside his bed. Reluctantly he started taking out his clothes, a blue suit, white shirt and a dark tie. Larren watched him for a moment, and then switched off the light and left him to dress in the dark. Mannering protested, but Larren warned him into silence and crossed to the window. He drew back the tall curtains and looked outside. The lawns and shrubbery below were dark and deserted, and immediately outside the window was a long balcony. Larren said softly:

"Can we get out this way?"

Mannering paused, fumbling with his tie.

"Yes," he said nervously. "There's a fire-escape ladder at the far end of the balcony that leads down into the grounds. But I think that window is locked."

He was right, but Larren could foresee too many difficulties in trying to take Mannering out by the same route he had used to get in, and so he busied himself with forcing the lock. It was no serious barrier to a man with his training, he had once attended a special course of lectures by an expert locksmith, and he had completed the task by the time Mannering had laced up his shoes.

Mannering pulled on a dark overcoat and joined him at the window. He hesitated again and there was still a subconscious wish to forestall the issue, for he said weakly:

"We haven't even been introduced."

Good God, Larren thought desperately. The man was mad. Smith was mad. He was mad. This was becoming a lunatics' party. He said aloud, but only just:

"My name is Simon Larren. That will have to do for now. Keep quiet and stay very close to me."

Mannering nodded unhappily, and together they moved along the balcony. Larren again had the Smith & Wesson in his hand, and was again praying that it would not be needed, not even as a threat. They reached the end of the balcony and descended the flight of steel rungs to the grounds, and taking Mannering's arm Larren led him through the darkness of the shrubbery away from the building. He cursed as the other man made clumsy rustling noises, and decided that however valuable Mannering might have been in diplomatic circles, he would be of very little use as an active agent in the field.

They reached the high, protective wall, and Larren whispered instructions. Mannering nodded once more, looked around uncertainly and then used Larren's bowed shoulders as a stepping stone to reach the top of the wall. Larren pushed him up, hissed at him to get over quickly, and then followed.

Mannering landed on the pavement beyond the wall and then froze rigid until Larren dropped down beside him. Larren had dropped the automatic into his pocket and now he left it there, for the side street was again deserted. He had to take Mannering's arm again and propel the man along beside him, stopping when they reached the corner and the main road.

A glance round the angle of the wall

showed no sign of the police guard on duty at the Institute gates, and Larren guessed that he was standing back in the gateway. He hesitated a moment, and then turned in the other direction and hurried Mannering along. It took them five minutes to reach the spot where he had arranged for Sharif to wait, and he breathed a sigh of relief when he saw a large black car waiting against the kerb. It was a bulky-looking Volga saloon, fairly old, and with taxi markings.

He wasted no time in bundling Mannering into the back seat, at the same time acknowledging the triumphant grin from Sharif who sat beside the driver. The Afghani said quietly:

"You are a little late. I was beginning to worry. Our friend beside me is getting suspicious."

Larren spared a glance for the taxi-driver, a small, uncertain man huddled into a heavy coat beneath a peaked cap. The panel light showed a worried mongoloid face, tightening with the first flicker of alarm as he heard his strange passengers speaking an unknown tongue.

Larren felt sorry for him. The man had been asked to wait for an ordinary fare, but tonight was not an ordinary night. Larren produced the Smith & Wesson again and touched the cold eye of the barrel to the frightened man's cheek. To Sharif he said grimly:

"Tell him to get driving as fast as he can. He may not have expected this, but he's taking us all the way to the frontier. Tell him that we won't hurt him unless we have to, and that it will make a nice change from driving fat commissars around Samarkand."

Sharif smiled and relayed the words. The unfortunate taxi-driver looked sideways, past the levelled automatic into the grey-green menace of Larren's eyes. Then he decided upon wholehearted co-operation and started the car.

The strike was successfully over, and they had only to make the fast return.

8

The Dust Peril

Under the threat of the gun the taxi-driver took them clear of Samarkand, but once they had reached a deserted stretch of the open road Larren forced him to stop. Mannering's face registered fear again and his body began to quake. He said tentatively:

"You're not — not going to kill him?"

Larren said grimly. "I don't see any need for that, yet. I'm just going to tie him up and dump him in the back seat with you. He's too slow and law abiding, and in any case, if anything goes wrong I'd rather that Sharif or myself was at the wheel."

Mannering said no more, but shifted farther into the corner of the back seat while the changeover was made. The terrified taxi-driver clearly thought that his last moments had come, despite

Sharif's assurances to the contrary, and he was visibly trembling as he got out of the car. Larren made him take off the grubby scarf he wore and used it to tie his hands. Then he pushed him into the back beside Mannering. Sharif shifted over behind the wheel and Larren took the seat beside him. The whole operation took only a few minutes, and then they were speeding on their way again. Sharif had the right sense of urgency, and forcing the car to the utmost he quickly regained the lost time.

After a few moments Sharif glanced at Larren and said:

"Perhaps you should have killed him. He may be a nuisance when we get nearer the frontier."

Larren said calmly: "If we kill him then we've got an unwanted body on our hands. We haven't got time to waste on concealing it effectively, and if we just dump him by the roadside he could be found and that would start the alarm. At the moment he's no more trouble alive than he would be dead, so we might as well take him with us in one piece. When we abandon the car we can leave him inside. We'll be back in Afghanistan before he can free himself and start screaming for help."

He smiled and added: "Besides, he's only a frightened little man, and I'm not a real bloodthirsty Afghani. He's probably got a lonely wife and a couple of little Mongol babies back home."

Sharif chuckled, showing no offence, and then concentrated on his driving.

They raced hard through the night, the sharp beam of the headlights thrusting over the long miles of asphalt and showing up brief glimpses of the barren desert on either side. They passed no other traffic on the road, and it seemed that the world was empty but for a few faint stars, the road and themselves. The big Volga was a powerful car and Sharif proved a reckless driver. Samarkand was soon far behind and after an hour Larren took over the wheel. Night driving at full speed was a strain on eyes and nerves, but by alternating at the wheel they expected to keep up the pace throughout the full two-hundred-mile drive.

In the back seat Mannering sat huddled and dejected, looking almost as sorry for himself as the forlorn little taxi-driver who was trussed up beside him. Larren found no time for any serious conversation as he handled the wheel, but occasionally he glanced up at Mannering's reflection in his rear view mirror and he wondered. Sharif, he sensed, was not over-impressed by their prize, and he too was growing dubious about the man behind him.

Until Smith had called him into the Whitehall office just over a week ago Larren had known no more about Nevile Mannering than had been blazed to the world in general by the newspapers. Mannering had been a highly placed civil servant, he had served terms abroad in several British embassies and had been well known in diplomatic circles. Then he had been suave and almost dapper, a greying English dandy moving in a world of cut-glass chandeliers, glittering receptions and cocktail parties. His defection to Moscow at the height of his career had provided perfect material for storm and scandal and the press had enjoyed a brief heyday with the minimum of facts and a maximum of speculation. Later came another flourish of headlines when it was revealed that Mannering had been a British espionage agent for the past ten years, but had turned double agent to spy for the Russians. According to reports he had been either suborned or blackmailed during a term of duty at the British Embassy in Moscow. When the double game became too risky he had fled to Russia for asylum.

The unpublicized part of the story was that of the double double-cross which Larren had heard from Smith. Mannering was playing the most dangerous game of all and was still working for British Counter Espionage, the department he had supposedly betrayed. For three years he had aligned himself with the Russians, working in close contact with the KGB and other Soviet security forces. His knowledge of their methods and their personnel would be invaluable to the West, and according to Smith he had the rare type of photographic mind that could store information away as accurately as any filing cabinet. Getting Mannering out had been high priority once his solitary, long-awaited contact had been made, but now it was obvious that Mannering did not want to come. Why?

Larren could think of a variety of answers to that. One was that Mannering had switched sides again. He had been a British agent, then a Russian agent, secretly still a British agent, and now why not another reverse to the Russians. There was no way of knowing what had really happened to him during the past three years, and at the best his loyalties must be confused and suspect. And in any case, regardless of his true loyalties, he could not expect to return to a hero's welcome. To convince the Russians that he was a genuine defector he must have betrayed at least some of his old comrades, men who were rated expendable, and no doubt a few who were not, as sacrifices on the altar of higher stakes. Larren had no illusions about espionage, and at best it was a dirty business where any man could become a pawn and the end always justified the means. The

KGB had been able to execute a quiet purge after Mannering's defection, and a number of British agents must have died. Smith might be satisfied with the returns, but there would be others who would hate Mannering's guts, and they would be men trained in murder.

After balancing the facts it was not surprising that Mannering had suffered a nervous breakdown. He had lived on his nerves for too long, and the appearance of a known killer such as Korovin at the Institute had proved the last straw. Or perhaps he had broken before that. He may have had second thoughts after making his signal for help and then told everything to the KGB. That would be the perfect explanation for Korovin's presence.

Larren glanced again at the dim reflection of Mannering's face in the mirror, and wondered what was really taking place in that once-calculating mind. He knew the story but he did not know the man. Was Mannering loyal to East or West, or merely to himself? Did he believe in God, in Communism, in justice or retribution? There was no way of knowing. There was no time to get inside the man and find out. He could only push on with his set task and get Mannering back to London. Smith could then take the man apart with a team of psychologists and sort out what was inside.

He had to defer his thinking when Sharif nudged his arm and pointed out that the petrol gauge was registering near to empty. The tank had been just over half full when they had started their journey, but they had now covered the first hundred miles. They had passed through two or three small townships, huddles of buildings that had swept past so swiftly that they were almost unnoticeable in the night, and Larren agreed that they would have to stop at the next opportunity to refuel.

The miles rushed by, another fifteen minutes passed, and then they saw the dim outlines of another sprawl of low houses appearing ahead. Larren slowed as they drove through the town, it appeared deserted and there was only one street light slung from a pole to illuminate the bare central square. They started to leave the town behind, but as the last of the buildings merged into the darkness beyond the beam of their lights, Sharif pointed out a single petrol pump standing before a tumbledown house at the roadside. Larren pulled off the road and stopped before the old-fashioned, hand-cranked pump. He switched off the engine and lights and then said:

"Tell our little man in the back that I've still got a gun in my hand. If he tries to escape or attract any attention then I won't hesitate to use it. He'll only succeed in getting the pump attendant killed and himself as well."

The words were addressed to Sharif, who translated then for the benefit of their prisoner in the back, but Larren made sure that they were also loud enough, and that his voice was hard enough to register with Mannering. He did not want to display his private doubts with a direct threat, but he wanted to be sure that Mannering understood the facts, and this was the best way.

There was no response from either of the occupants of the back seat, and Larren waited while Sharif got out and went over to the stone-built house behind the pump. The Afghani pounded noisily on the door with his fist, and after several minutes succeeded in rousing a protesting head at an upper window. A vigorous argument followed, but Sharif was obviously refusing to either go away or wait until dawn, and finally the grumbling proprietor consented to serve them.

Sharif came back to the car, grinning confidently, and after another short delay the man who had been at the window appeared. He was wrapped up in an ancient ex-army greatcoat and continued to mutter and curse as he unlocked the petrol pump and proceeded to fill up the tank. It was a slow job and after ten gallons had been pumped into the car Sharif allowed him to stop and paid him. The tank was still not full, but there was more than enough to get them to the frontier.

As Sharif got back inside Larren started

the engine and drove off. As they bumped back on to the road he said quietly:

"Is he likely to report us? A Samarkand taxi this far south must make him a little curious."

"I think not." Sharif sounded confident. "I told him that our passenger's sister has been suddenly taken ill in Termez, and I think he is satisfied with that explanation. In any case there were no telephone wires leading from the house, so he would have to walk back into town to report any suspicions. At this time of night I think he will prefer to go back to his bed."

They settled down to drive once more, maintaining their headlong flight through the darkness. There was a silent atmosphere of tension in the car that began to get worse as they clocked up the miles towards Termez. Mannering was scared but resigned, and did not speak throughout the whole journey. He nursed his fears and did not even ask how they intended to get him across the frontier. Sharif was grim-faced, his lips set beneath the eagle-hooked nose. When he next relieved Larren at the wheel he smiled faintly, but that was all. They stayed alert, driving fast, and hoping that Mannering's escape would not be noticed until dawn.

The road began to climb up into the low mountains, but Sharif did not slacken speed. The big Volga swayed dangerously as he flung it around the bends, shredding rubber from tyres that shrieked in protest. Larren hoped that the tyre pressures were correct and that they had started off with plenty of tread. A blowout at this stage would be fatal.

They slowed up to pass through the small town that marked the highest point of the road, and then began the descent to the last fifty miles of barren plains before Termez. Sharif pressed on the accelerator and they continued their breakneck speed.

Larren could feel his own nerves tightening now, and he borrowed the map on which Sharif had marked the approximate positions of the two checkpoints along this last stretch of road. He kept a careful watch on the mileage indicator, and when he calculated that they would soon be approaching the first checkpoint he gave Sharif the order to turn off into the desert.

Their fast, smooth progress ended as they left the road, and now their flight entered the more hazardous final lap. The car lurched and jolted over the hard, stony earth, and they had to gamble against the increased possibility of a burst tyre or broken spring. They had to circle wide around the two checkpoints, for they could not be sure how far the sound of their engine might carry across the desert. The unknown factors of hearing distance and the exact locations of the checkpoints added to the taunt atmosphere, for the lack of time prevented them from making too wide a safety margin with their circular route. They had made excellent time, but now their speed was reduced by half and dawn was less than two hours away.

Larren took over the wheel again, straining his eyes into the gloom to avoid the gulleys, rocks and bushes that littered the desert. The bright beam of the headlights would be visible for miles and he preferred to switch them off now that they had left the road. Beside him Sharif was free to concentrate on the heavens, navigating their course by the stars.

They had turned right off the road, driving five miles into the desert and then turning due left to make a direct line south to the frontier. They had to avoid the checkpoints and the frontier town of Termez, so they had no intention of returning to the road. The drive turned into a cross-country scramble with Larren desperately trying to maintain an average of fifteen miles per hour. The car was taking a battering and they were all being badly shaken up, but they were still twenty miles short of the frontier and he was being forced to race against the coming dawn.

The dust storm blew up suddenly. The wind strengthened, slapping around the car, and then the dust swirled up before them. Sharif swore as in a matter of minutes the night sky was blotted from his view. The car rocked and swayed under the powerful gusts of wind that threatened to roll it over, and Larren echoed Sharif's cursing as he was forced to take his foot from the accelerator. He could see nothing and the Volga crashed and lurched as the offside wheel mounted some hidden obstruction, either a bush or a rock. Angrily Larren braked and stopped the car.

For a moment he could only stare at the thick fog of dust and sand that rushed across the windscreen. The wind was howling and dashing the sand against the car's flanks in an abrasive fury that threatened to rub the paintwork down to the bare steel. They were enveloped in a blinding nightmare that had all the massive forces of spiteful nature ranged against them.

Mannering said wretchedly: "I thought something like this would happen. This is the finish. By the time the storm passes it will be daylight. Korovin will find that I'm missing and he'll telephone all the frontier posts to stop us."

Larren ignored him and asked harshly: "How long can this go on?"

"Hours perhaps." Sharif bit his lip and then added: "Switch on the headlights.

It won't matter now. Perhaps we can continue."

Larren realized that the Afghani was right. No one would be able to pick out the beam of their headlights amongst all this flying muck. He switched them on, but all he got was a clearer picture of the millions of dust and sand particles that tumbled through the groping double beam. He hesitated, and then looked again at Sharif.

"How much farther to the frontier?"

"About ten miles. Possibly less."

"Then I'll push on. If I wreck the car we'll have to try it on foot. There's no future in sitting here."

Sharif nodded. Larren shifted into gear again and began driving slowly forward. The wind increased its wild efforts to blow the car over, making it lurch drunkenly from side to side, but Larren tightened his mouth and ignored it. He could see only occasional glimpses of the terrain ahead as the dust clouds raced past, and he braced himself to meet the shock of crashing over the obstacles he could not distinguish in time to

149

avoid. The speedometer needle flickered between five and ten miles per hour, and at this speed even if he smashed the car headlong into a house-sized boulder they should all escape unhurt. His big fear was that they might plunge into some deep gulley or ravine, but there had been no serious fractures in the earth before the dust storm appeared, and he could only hope that that state of affairs would continue.

His luck held out for almost six miles, crawling blindly through the sand-filled night. The Volga was a sturdily made saloon and suffered a violent amount of punishment, but mercilessly collided with nothing large enough to stop its progress. When the inevitable happened it was not a dead stop and a shattering crash, but instead a slewing movement to one side and a helpless spinning of the rear wheels. The back end of the car sank and Larren realized grimly that he had bogged down in a patch of soft sand. He cursed, but they had no other choice but to abandon the car.

Mannering's nerve had crumbled and

Larren had to force him to get out of the car. He had to be ruthless now and he was glad that Sharif was still a pillar of support beside him. They would need the Afghani's inbuilt sense of direction to keep moving due south to the frontier. They tied handkerchiefs around their faces to protect themselves from the choking dust and then linked hands. With their heads bowed and Sharif leading they struggled on through the howling sand blizzard on foot.

The little taxi-driver they left still bound in the shelter of the car. When the storm cleared later in the day he would no doubt be found and released, but by then it would be too late to have any deciding effect upon their own fate. They had to reach the Oxus before dawn, or at least before the storm cleared, otherwise their chances of escape were nil.

9

Desert Trek

Simon Larren had been in some tough places during his long and varied career, but this present experience was the nearest that he had ever encountered to a foretaste of pure, undiluted hell. Sealed inside the car it had been bad enough, but once they stepped out into the open the wind became a savage, screaming fury that seemed bent on nothing less than their total destruction. They had taken barely three fumbling steps before the car was swamped from their view, lost in the hideous dust clouds behind them as though it had never existed. The handkerchief that they had tied around their faces were practically useless against the driving sand that forced its way viciously into their eyes, mouths and nostrils. They were blind, choking, suffocating, and showers of tiny stones

152

caught up in the winds bombarded them like swarms of flying meteors in some science fiction nightmare.

Mannering stumbled and hung back, gasping that it was impossible, and Larren and Sharif had to drag him along between them. Larren had one arm wrapped around his bowed face, and his free hand gripping fast to Mannering's sleeve. Sharif had adopted the same posture, while Mannering had both arms flung up to protect his face. They could see nothing, so they kept their eyes tightly closed. If they opened their mouths to speak they were forced to swallow mouthfuls of the gritty, penetrating sand, and so they struggled in silence. Mannering's initial protests had been quickly choked off. The wind strove to knock them over and they had to fight to stay on their feet.

Larren had no idea of how long or how far they travelled. He lost all sense of time and distance and had to concentrate on simply keeping moving. Mannering tugged like a dead weight on his arm, and unseen bushes and boulders joined the sporting wind gleefully in trying to trip him up and bowl him over. His own senses were useless now and he had to trust implicitly to Sharif. They might have been wandering around in circles but he had faith in the Afghani's sense of direction. It was the only thing he could cling to. Mannering, he knew, had already given up hope, and was probably praying for death.

They fell a great number of times, sometimes individually, sometimes together, cursing and gathering a wide collection of cuts, grazes and bruises. Larren stopped counting the number of falls, stopped thinking altogether, except to reflect that he was now suffering with a vengeance for all the good luck that had favoured him on the outward run.

They began to weaken, beaten into submission by the sheer force of the wind, and then abruptly all three tripped and crashed down in the most violent fall yet. Larren and Sharif went headlong together and Mannering was dragged down behind them. Instinct opened Larren's eyes and he was just in time to twist his neck and avoid dashing his head against a length of steel rail. Mannering uttered a deflating cry as the parallel rail; the one that had tripped Larren and Sharif, smashed him hard across the chest. Larren had an agonizing pain where he had cracked his shin, but it was eased by a rush of pure relief. They had found the railway tracks that ran close to the frontier.

He forced his eyes to remain open in narrow slits, squinting to assure himself that they had indeed found the tracks. Sharif was struggling up slowly, but Mannering still lay groaning across the first rail. Larren started to rise to help him, but then he realized something else. It was no longer night, the darkness had receded and they were now enveloped in rushing clouds of greyish-yellow. While they had walked with their eyes closed the dawn had overtaken them.

He could not even be sure how far the dawn was advanced. By now Korovin may have already discovered that Mannering was gone and a swift telephone call would alert the border guards.

Larren faltered under a wave of despair, and then just as quickly forced it down.

Daylight was not the disaster it might have been, for the sand storm that had delayed them might now save their lives. Korovin could alert as many patrols as he liked, but no one would find them in this. While the storm lasted there was still a chance.

He pulled Mannering up and urged the man on. Sharif was perhaps the fittest of them all for he even managed a brief smile above the handkerchief mask that had slipped when he fell. They left the tracks behind and soon came to the road which they remembered from their previous frontier crossing. The wind was lessening now and the swirling dust was not so thick, and Larren knew that they had very little time. They hurried faster and Mannering began sobbing from the pain in his chest that constricted his breathing.

Visibility was lengthening with every minute, and then through the dust cloud Larren saw the ominous shape of one of the frontier watchtowers rising ahead. He hissed a warning to Sharif and they swung away to one side, running now as they covered the last stretch of Russian soil. The barbed-wire fence reared up before them and they knelt down before it with wildly beating hearts. Mannering collapsed but for the moment they allowed him to lay unattended. The storm was dying, the curtain of dust becoming thinner with every second, and at any moment they could become fully visible to the guards on the watchtower.

Larren's hands were fast and feverish, but his brain ordered icy control. He pulled the wire cutters out of his pocket, and very deftly snapped through the lower strands of the fence. Sharif pulled the cut wires away and they literally pushed Mannering through the gap. Sharif followed and Larren came last. This time he could not afford to stop and repair the wire behind him and he hurried after Sharif.

They reached the end of the sand cliffs that lined the river bank, hesitating in search of a way down. Here the cliff was no more than fifteen feet high and there was a level beach at the bottom. The nearest watchtower was emerging fast from the retreating clouds of yellow dust and Larren said curtly:

"Jump!"

Sharif nodded, bracing one hand momentarily on the sandy edge that crumbled away as he dropped out into space. He fell as he landed in a flurry of spurting sand, but quickly scrambled up again and moved clear. Mannering hesitated, but Larren gave him a ruthless shove and he had no choice. He sat down on the cliff edge with his legs dangling, and before he could hesitate again the edge gave way and he fell out of sight.

Larren followed them down, landing with a classical paratroop roll. The shock to his legs hardly bothered him and he was up in a moment. Sharif was unharmed, but Mannering was groaning audibly. He sat where he had fallen, and when Sharif helped him up he limped badly.

They were out of sight of the tower now and for a minute they could relax. Despite his limp Mannering had no bones broken, and Larren decided that he was more shaken up than anything. He forgot his limp almost immediately as he stared at the dark flood of the Oxus that surged past only a few yards away and said weakly:

"Good God, how are we going to cross that?"

"We swim." Larren was already stripping off his clothes. "That's the way Sharif and I arrived, so it's not impossible."

Mannering was shattered, his horror was complete. His eyes were raw and bloodshot from the stinging dust and the prospect of this new ordeal filled them with tears.

"Larren, you're mad. You and your friend might be able to cross that river, but not me. I don't swim very well. I'll never do it."

Larren felt a genuine surge of pity, but he could not let it last. Pity was something he dared not tolerate, for the Oxus had to be crossed. He made his voice stay curt and said:

"You can't turn back now. Once across the river you'll be safe, and Sharif and I are here to help you. Once again you'll just have to rely on us."

Mannering looked wretched, but after a moment he nodded and began to strip off his coat. He had been resigned to dying in the sand blizzard and now he was resigned to dying in the river. His mind was in torment and death would be a welcome release.

All three of them stripped naked. Mannering's heavy overcoat they had to discard, but the rest of their clothing they divided into two bundles, again protected by the waterproof sheets, which Larren and Sharif strapped to their backs. The two heavy turbans they now unravelled and used as an improvised lifeline, linking themselves together with Mannering in the middle. Weakening swirls of dust still stung their bodies as they prepared, and they shivered against the morning cold. Larren had no more of the channel-swimming grease to coat their limbs, and he could only hope that they would not freeze before they reached the far bank.

Mannering baulked again at the water's edge. His white body was running to fat and he looked pathetic as his limbs quaked. However, once they had left the shelter of the cliff they could not dither. They had to enter the water quickly and once the hungry river had them in its grip there was no turning back. Again the shock stopped Larren's heart and lungs as he was dragged under, and whether or not they had been seen during their quick rush across the open beach became abruptly irrelevant. A hail of bullets from the watchtower would have been almost a blessing during those first paralysing moments.

That second crossing of the Oxus was far more terrifying than the first. They had already exhausted much of their strength in fighting their way through the dust storm, and now Larren and Sharif had the extra burden of Mannering dragging at the makeshift rope around their waists. At first Larren had the horrible fear that the icy plunge had caused Mannering to have a heart attack, and that they were towing a dead man. Then he realized that Mannering was alive and struggling to swim beside him. The Oxus seemed faster, wider, deeper, and more freezing than before, and they fought another desperate battle for their lives in its hostile embrace.

Once again they were being carried rapidly downstream, like helpless drift-wood caught up in the racing current. Mannering floundered like some panic-stricken baby whale, his gasping face turning blue with cold as he fought to stay afloat, but it was left to Larren and Sharif to make gradual headway towards the far bank. Larren was tiring, yet he had hopes that his strength would last out, there were still untapped reservoirs in his flagging muscles. What frightened him was the excruciating sub-zero cold that was biting through to the very core of his being. He tried to imagine the Oxus in midsummer when it would be in full flood from the snows melting in the mountains, and knew that then it would be impassable. Even now it might prove to be his grave.

Without Sharif it would have been a grave, a last Afghani place for both Larren and Mannering. Only the Afghani lasted for the full distance, and when he reached his home shore he had to drag both Englishmen up the beach behind him. Larren was more dead than alive, his limbs numbed and barely capable of movement, while Mannering was unconscious. During the last few yards Larren had possessed just enough instinct for survival to hold both his own and Mannering's head above water, and Sharif had fought the final battle alone.

The Afghani had almost reached his own point of exhaustion during the last gruelling minutes, but he still had the presence of mind to move both his companions over the first sand dune where they could lay out of sight of the watchtowers on the Soviet bank. Larren sprawled face down on the sand and felt Sharif pulling away the pack from his shoulders. Then he was rolled over and Sharif was forcing the hard neck of a flask between his lips. He tasted brandy and choked. A trickle of warmth cracked the ice that had formed in his bloodstream and the pain was unbearable. More brandy was forced down his throat and slowly he felt the cold hand of death relax on his heart.

Sharif was satisfied that he would live and left him to attend Mannering. Larren was incapable of giving any help and could only lay drained and helpless in the sand, but after what seemed like an eternity Sharif said wearily:

"Mister Mannering is at least alive. I think we can say that our mission has been a success."

★ ★ ★

An hour passed before they were able to make any real move. Sharif unfastened the sodden rope of cloth that linked them all together, and then he and Larren used their shirts to rub their frozen bodies dry before wriggling thankfully into the rest of their clothes. Then they did their best for Mannering. The older man was still unconscious, half-drowned and blue with cold, but they dried him and dressed him, and then gingerly trickled the rest of the brandy down his throat. After that they had to lay in the sand dunes and rest, building up their strength once more and allowing the rising sun to thaw out their still-numbed bones. Mannering recovered, shivering and with chattering teeth, and Larren wondered if he would survive the obvious dangers of pneumonia. They needed more rest to fully restore their strength, but Mannering needed to move to keep warm, and so after that first hour had passed they resolutely faced the need to resume their flight.

The day was now well advanced, and they had to crouch low as they moved deeper into the dunes, away from the Oxus. When they were out of sight of the watchtowers on the Soviet bank they straightened up, turned to the east and began the long weary trek across the desert that would take them back to the main road. They knew that there was no point in searching for their nomad guide who would have been waiting during the hours of darkness with their three horses. By now the man would have taken them back to the nomad camp, and they could not afford to delay another twelve to fourteen hours until he returned again to his nightly vigil. They had mis-timed their re-entry into Afghanistan, and now they had to walk.

The very fact that they had succeeded in getting out of Soviet Russia cheered their spirits, but Larren knew that Sharif might well be premature in assuming that their mission was already a success. Russian influence was effective even on this side of the Oxus, the KGB was well established, and Mannering could not be considered wholly safe until they had flown him completely clear of Afghanistan. Larren cursed the fact that they had so narrowly missed their rendezvous with the waiting horses, for the hours they were wasting now might well prove vital before they reached Kabul.

The sun was warm, and even Mannering rallied a little at the start of their long walk. After the dust storm and the river the rolling dunes seemed an easy barrier to cross, but very soon fatigue was reaching out to drag them down. They had not yet regained a tenth of the energy they had expended during the course of the night, and so it was not long before their brief revival began to fade. The sand dunes became another ordeal, the desert another implacable enemy.

Predictably Mannering was the first to give way, and they had to stop frequently for the older man to rest. Sharif calculated that they could be anything between five and fifteen miles from the road, and the uncertainty did not help. Mannering would have lain down and died, but Larren would not allow him that final relief. The sun climbed higher, and Mannering had to be supported to make him move at all. Larren and Sharif had his arms around their shoulders and half-carried him along. Ironically they began to sweat, where just over two hours previously they had been in grave danger of freezing to death. Afghanistan was a land of extremes.

Sharif was fortunately accustomed to the conditions of his own land, his endurance seemed unlimited and he continued to prove the strongest of them all. Larren's mind again became a blank, he stopped worrying and thinking, and devoted all that was left inside him into supporting Mannering and the endless task of pushing his feet forward across the equally endless desert. Sharif was their eyes, ears and guiding brain. Without the Afghani they would have been lost.

Time again became meaningless, distance vague, and the world had resolved into a drab, continuing film of yellow hills of sand. There were a few patches of grass and stunted bushes, but nothing that could really break the burning monotony. Thirst began to add another ironic touch to their suffering. After they had almost drowned nature was having a gigantic joke at their expense.

The end came suddenly. The sun was directly above them and they had been marching east for at least four to five hours, and then Sharif brought them to a stumbling halt. Mannering sagged between them and was totally spent, but Larren managed to lift his head and open his eyes. His vision was blurred but he saw that they had reached the road. He swallowed hard but nothing would come, no words, no relief, no joy. His mouth was too dry and his body was sapped even of emotion.

Sharif said hoarsely:

"The encampment where we left Asefi with the Land Rover is still a long way south of us. We must take a chance and beg a lift from the next vehicle to use the road. Now that we are back in my own country it should be safe."

Larren forced his mind to function, trying to grasp and analyse the new situation. The position of the sun told him that it was past noon. By now Mannering must have been missed from the Lenin Institute. The alarm would be raised. It was possible that their abandoned car had been found, and there had been time for another fast car to make the two-hundred-mile drive from Samarkand to Termez. Afghan-Soviet relations were good and any pursuit would have the advantage of being able to cross the Oxus directly by the bridge at Termez, with possibly only the briefest delay for paperwork and control regulations. They were bleak thoughts, and Larren had to make an effort to move his dry tongue.

"I agree that we have to take a chance — but don't wave down any big, black, official-looking cars. We might find ourselves welcomed by a very nasty character named Korovin."

10

The Best Laid Plans

They lowered Mannering to the ground, sat down beside him, and could do nothing then but wait at the roadside for the next half-hour. Then the unaccountable mood of fate that seemed to be for them at one moment and against them the next relented and granted them another stroke of luck. The next vehicle to appear from the direction of Termez was not a large black saloon filled with avenging agents of the KGB, but an ordinary lorry lumbering through a screen of its own churned-up dust. It was a high, square-built truck of Soviet make, but its wooden sides were painted with the gay, flamboyant colours so beloved by Afghani drivers. In a western museum it might well have been accepted as a work of modern art.

Sharif flagged it down and went forward to hold an earnest discussion with the driver. The man seemed to hesitate as he leaned down from the wheel, but then he nodded and Sharif climbed up into the cab. It had already been decided that if possible Larren and Mannering would climb into the back where they would not prompt too many questions from the driver, and on receiving a signal from Sharif Larren helped the older man to get aboard. There was a steel-runged ladder just behind the cab to help them scale the high sides, but even then Mannering almost didn't make it. Larren had to shove him from behind and he practically fell into the back of the lorry. Larren joined him and helped him to sit with his back against the cab, and then the lorry jolted on its way.

The lorry was empty, so they were treated to a fast but uncomfortable ride. Mannering was in very bad shape and Larren had to support him all the way, holding him upright so that the shaking of the lorry did not roll him over. Fortunately it was only a short ride and after half an hour the lorry rattled to a stop. Larren could see nothing but the enclosing wooden walls, but he could hear Sharif dismounting and thanking their driver, and knew that they had returned to the site of the nomad encampment.

He had more difficulty in getting Mannering out of the lorry, and Sharif had to climb up the outside ladder to help him. After a struggle they got the man down on to the road, and with a doubtful farewell wave from the driver the big wheels turned up more dust and the lorry snorted on its way. Sharif watched it go and then said grimly:

"That man is suspicious. His lorry was thoroughly searched when he came through the frontier, and he could not avoid noticing Mannering's condition and his western clothes. I do not think that he will talk with anyone, except to gossip with other drivers in the *Chai* houses, but even so I think we must waste as little time as possible in getting back to Kabul."

Larren was in full agreement, for he needed no convincing that their position was still a dangerous one. They turned away from the road, again helping Mannering between them, and began the last short walk across the desert to where they could already see the low black tents of the nomads.

Their approach did not escape notice and Asefi came to meet them with some of the younger men from the camp. The little man still looked too small for his turban and had another *Lucky Strike* adhering to his lip. He smiled widely at their return and asked a barrage of quick, excited questions. Sharif could only manage short, weary answers, but Asefi was not perturbed. Some of their escort took over the task of supporting Mannering, and Larren and Sharif were able to straighten their aching backs and walk unemcumbered into the camp.

The old greybeard who ruled the community was standing upright with some of his elders to greet them. Sharif conferred with the old man for several minutes, and Larren was relieved when they were invited to sit down. His legs were almost collapsing beneath him and he subsided gratefully on to the sand. He wanted badly to sleep, but he had to stay polite and awake while Sharif continued talking to the nomads.

An incongruous tea-party developed. They sat crosslegged in a circle and the tea was served sweet and scalding hot in small, fragile glasses. To Larren's parched lips it was nectar, as blissful as anything he had ever tasted. An old woman shrouded and veiled in black had appeared to tend the big kettle that was boiling on the fire, and silently she refilled the tiny glasses. Food was brought, a simple meal of goat's cheese and unleavened bread, but Larren found that he was ravenous and this time he had no fear of offending the hospitality of these people by being reluctant to accept his share.

Asefi had left to fetch the Land Rover. It had been hidden deeper in the desert out of sight of the road, and by the time they had eaten and rested they heard the familiar sound of the engine and saw the Land Rover bouncing towards them with Asefi grinning behind the wheel. He stopped close beside the huddle of tents and waited, content to be back in the driving seat where he belonged.

Mannering was still in a dazed and exhausted condition. He had managed to swallow several glasses of the hot tea, but had eaten nothing and for all practical purposes was in a state of collapse. Sharif suggested that they make him a rough bed in the back of the Land Rover, and then proceeded to bargain tactfully for some blankets from their hosts. He finally managed to purchase three that were greasy and probably flea-ridden, but remarked somewhat callously that by the time Mannering was strong enough to worry about a few fleas he would also be strong enough to throw the blankets away.

They made the sick man comfortable and then shook hands and said their farewells to the nomads. Sharif managed the delicate matter of paying the balance due for the many services rendered, and the old greybeard solemnly handed the exchanged notes to one of his advisers for counting. Larren and Sharif joined Asefi in the Land Rover, and the men of the desert watched them depart with proud and unspeculative faces. Then they went about their ordinary, everyday business.

On the road to the south Larren and Sharif thankfully relaxed and left Asefi to do the driving. Sharif folded his arms across his chest, closed his eyes, and with no difficulty fell asleep. Mannering had passed out under his blankets in the back, but Simon Larren had to stay awake for just a little while longer. They reached the large town of Mazar-i-Sharif, and Asefi stopped the Land Rover while Larren got out to make a telephone call.

After a ten-minute delay he heard Caroline Brand's acknowledging voice from Kabul. He said quietly:

"The word is *strikefast*. Estimated time of arrival, approximately thirty hours from now."

There was a pause, and then Caroline answered calmly:

"Understood — and congratulations."

Larren smiled tiredly and replaced the phone. He went back to the Land Rover, and now he too could sleep while Asefi drove them home.

Larren's estimation was not far out. Asefi had been impressed with the still urgent need for speed and he drove the Land Rover flat-out on the homeward journey. By nightfall he had reached Haibak, and they were able to stop overnight at the small *chai* house that had accommodated them only four nights previously on their way north. They started out again an hour before dawn and Asefi put in another twelve hours of hard, concentrated driving, with only short stops to eat and stretch their cramped muscles. The Land Rover climbed back through the giant, mountain barrier of the Hindu Kush, leaving the deserts far behind to enter the icy heights, and at about noon they again passed through the lofty tunnel of the Salang Pass. They descended towards the valley of the Kabul River, and at dusk they were again re-entering the capital city of Afghanistan.

Larren felt incredibly tired, and yet at the same time he had regained much of his lost strength. Every muscle in his body felt as though it had been crushed and congealed into absolute weariness, but he felt that once he could move and loosen out some of the stiffness caused by the long hours of driving then he would begin to revert to his normal fitness. Beside him Sharif appeared to be fully recovered from their flight across the frontier, and gave the impression that catching up on lost sleep in a sitting position in a wildly driven Land Rover was mere child's play. Behind them Mannering was still an invalid under his blankets, but he was getting stronger and over the worst effects of his ordeal.

Asefi had cut down on his speed on the last lap across the Kabul valley. Swirls of mist were competing with the fading light in destroying visibility. Asefi switched on his headlights, rubbed a hand momentarily across his eyes, and then concentrated more earnestly on the road. Larren glanced at the little man and saw that he was feeling the long strain of driving, but he did not interfere. He knew that Asefi would not be willing to relinquish the wheel. The mist thickened into a dense fog and Asefi peeled the wrapper off a stick of chewing gum with one hand and his teeth, pushing the gum into his mouth. Chewing seemed to aid his concentration.

Their progress was cut to a crawl when they entered Kabul, and the beam of their lights made a feeble grey thrust that barely penetrated through the restless blanket of vapour that filled the streets. Larren felt the rise of frustration. First a dust storm and now the fog. It seemed that nature was definitely not on his side. However, at least they had reached Kabul, and despite the difficulties Asefi found his way to the road that ran outside Caroline Brand's apartment.

Asefi switched off the engine and they climbed thankfully out of the cab of the Land Rover. The night was bitterly cold and Larren and Sharif lost no time in helping Mannering to get out of the back. Their prize was weak and unsteady, his pasty face looking white and ill, but he insisted that he could now walk unaided. Larren did not argue with him but led the way into the courtyard and then up the flight of steps to reach Caroline's apartment. He raised his hand to knock, but she had been alert and waiting, and the door was pulled open before his fist could fall.

All four of them pressed inside, Asefi standing respectfully back against the wall, while Larren and Sharif guided Mannering into a chair. Caroline closed the door and turned to face them. Her face showed a mixture of relief and concern, and she ignored Larren's faint smile and Sharif's grin as she saw the broken appearance of Mannering.

"Simon, what the hell have you done to him?"

"Quite a lot," Larren said regretfully. "That nervous breakdown was genuine. That was why he was at the Samarkand Institute. He's been living on his nerves for a long time, and getting him out wasn't quite as easy as we had hoped. He's had a tough time all round."

"I've got another bottle of whisky," Caroline said practically. "I think you all look as though you need a good strong dose. After that coffee, some food, and then we can talk."

Sharif said politely: "Just the coffee and food for me, please. No alcohol. I think the same applies for Asefi."

Caroline nodded. She produced another bottle of *Old Kentucky* and Larren assumed that Ray Gastoni had made another call. She poured three strong drinks for herself, Larren and Mannering, and then turned away into the kitchen. She had prepared for their arrival and the coffee-pot was already on the boil. She had even cut a great pile of beef sandwiches and Larren smiled in appreciation. She had thought of everything. He was still enjoying the warming glow of the whisky, and he knew his first question was irrelevant even before he asked:

"Is everything organized?"

She nodded, opened a drawer and flipped two British passports on the table. Larren's own and Mannering's.

"They are all ready. The plane tickets are inside them. You are both booked on the evening flight to New Delhi with

Ariana Afghan Airways. The flight was scheduled to take off in just over an hour's time, just too convenient to be true. You would have been safely in New Delhi before midnight, and there's even a BOAC connection to London tomorrow morning." She paused wryly and added: "There's just one snag."

Larren knew. "The fog."

Caroline nodded. "That's right, Simon. The best laid plans of mice and men, and all that jazz. All flights from Kabul airport have been grounded until further notice. That means until the fog clears."

"Blast." Larren glanced at Sharif. "Do you think it will clear by morning?"

The young Afghani shrugged. "Who knows? Perhaps yes, perhaps no. A fog as dense as this might linger for two or three days."

Larren felt like cursing, but Caroline forestalled him by saying in the same wry tone:

"And that's not the worst of our troubles, Simon. There's more."

Larren stared up into her level blue eyes, and knew that she was trying to break hard news gently. He said:

"Tell me."

Caroline sat on the edge of the table. The others were seated around her, hesitant in the acts of eating or drinking. Mannering looked scared, Sharif politely interested, and Asefi uncertain because he did not understand exactly what was going on. Caroline told Larren frankly:

"I had a telephone call this afternoon from Ray Gastoni. He has a contact at the airport who keeps him notified of anything that might be of interest. Apparently a private plane landed from the Soviet Union just before the fog closed the airport. It had flown direct from Tashkent, which is Russia's international airport terminus north of Samarkand. It landed three men, and one of them was a name with which you might be familiar, a KGB agent named Korovin."

This time Larren did curse. Then he explained grimly:

"Korovin was at the Lenin Institute in Samarkand, keeping a close watch on Mannering. Somehow they knew that there was a move afoot to pull him out. So if Korovin is now here in Kabul then obviously he's hoping to get Mannering back. He must have realized that we would try to reach the international airport here in order to fly Mannering out of Afghanistan." He stood up and began to pace about the room as he finished bitterly. "Korovin didn't even have to chase us across the frontier. He flew here ahead of us. And you can bet that the two boys with him were not just ordinary travellers. Korovin's a killer and he's brought some heavy support."

Sharif had listened intently. Now he asked:

"What will you do now?"

Larren was silent for a moment, and then he said:

"If we wait for the fog to lift then we give Korovin time to get organized. At the best we won't get a flight out of Kabul until sometime tomorrow morning, and by then he'll have worked out some means of stopping us at the airport. I don't think he'd try violence and an armed snatch there, but at the same time I don't think he'll find that necessary. Mannering has entered the country illegally and he'll be using a monkeyed-up passport. Normally it would get him through, but not if the airport officials are prewarned. This blasted fog gives Korovin time to make too many telephone calls and too many contacts. Which means that we have to change our plans and find an alternative escape route. The airport is too obvious and too dangerous."

Caroline smoothed a wave of dark gold hair away from her right eye and asked:

"What exactly do you have in mind?"

Larren replied honestly: "I don't know yet, but now that Korovin has entered the field we are going to need come extra help. And whether Ray Gastoni likes it or not I'm going to have to break that promise to keep him uninvolved."

11

Dead Men Do No Favours

Caroline said bluntly: "Ray isn't going to like that."

Larren grimaced. "That's too bad, but he's supposed to be co-operating on this job. Getting Mannering out is important, and now that we've succeeded this far I don't think he'll be prepared to refuse. The CIA wouldn't thank him for that. Even if he won't take any active part in helping us, he can still provide some ideas. This is his home ground, and with the airport closed he should know the next best way of getting a man out of the country."

Caroline nodded her head dubiously, and then asked:

"Shall I call him?"

She reached for the telephone but Larren stopped her.

"No, there's too much risk in asking

him to come here. Remember that Korovin arrived in Kabul before we did. The automatic thing for him to do would be to send a man out to the road from the north to watch out for our arrival. There's just a slim possibility that we were picked up and followed here. In this fog a convoy could have trailed our rear lights and we would never have known. If this building is compromised then we could be asking Gastoni to walk into a trap."

Sharif said quietly: "If you wish, I will contact Ray."

"No, I think I'd better do that job myself. As Caroline has pointed out he isn't going to be in full favour of any extra co-operation. I may have to argue with him for half the night. You had best stay here and take care of Caroline and Mannering. Just tell me where I can contact Gastoni."

It was Sharif's turn to be hesitant, for he knew he was breaking his friend's security. But after a moment he said reluctantly:

"Ray has a permanent room in the

Pamir Hotel. From here you go back to your own hotel, the Spinzar, cross the Kabul River, follow the road and cross the main avenue through the old part of the city, and you will find the Pamir Hotel on the edge of the bazaar. It is not a very elaborate place, and Ray's room is number seventeen on the second floor." He paused and then added: "Of course, I cannot guarantee that Ray will be there. He has responsibilities to his construction job which frequently takes him out of Kabul."

"He telephoned me this afternoon," Caroline reminded them. "It's unlikely that he'll have left in the fog."

Larren was not so certain. Gastoni would realize that the fog would mean complications, and if he had decided to shirk any responsibility he could quite easily have pulled out of Kabul for a few days. However, he did not rate Gastoni as a coward, but more as a stubborn, blustering character who simply did not like an operation on which he was only half-informed. There was a hard shrewdness under Gastoni's façade, and if he could be persuaded to join them then Larren knew that the American would be a useful man to have around. The only way to find out was to make a visit to the Pamir Hotel.

Larren was now wearing his normal western suit, for the dark stain had begun to disappear from his face and hands and he had thankfully changed out of his Afghani disguise during the overnight stop at Haibak. Now he unbuttoned his dark grey jacket, and took out the Smith & Wesson .38 automatic. He tossed it over to Caroline, who caught it neatly and said:

"You'd better have this. If the opposition are on to us then you should be able to take care of Mannering while I'm away. You've got Sharif to help you, and he just about equals a small army."

Sharif smiled at the compliment and said: "It is the natural result of being born an Afghani."

Caroline did not look so happy. She checked over the automatic with the reflex of a professional, but her eyes were troubled as she looked at Larren.

190

"What about you, Simon. If there is somebody out there?"

Larren smiled briefly. "It's night, remember. A dark, swirling foggy night with practically no visibility. It may be detrimental to aeroplanes, but it's tailored to order for me."

There was nothing more to be said. Larren finished his coffee and the last of the *Old Kentucky* in his glass, and then put on his overcoat. They moved the resigned and hapless Mannering into the greater safety of the bedroom and sent Asefi with him, and then switched off the lights. Sharif opened the door and Larren moved out into the fog and darkness.

The door closed quickly behind him and silently he moved to his left along the balcony. The steps he would have normally used were to his right, but Larren had played these games too often to make the obvious mistakes. He listened for a moment, heard and saw nothing, and then moved deftly over the balcony rail. He lowered himself down, dropped into the courtyard below, and for the second time remained motionless in the freezing fog.

There was still nothing to alarm him and he walked slowly towards the foot of the balcony stairs. There was no one waiting there and he could have strolled down quite calmly in the usual manner. However, he was unperturbed. He had needed the exercise and it was worth making a fool of himself occasionally just to stay in practice. The next time that such a roundabout route saved his life would not be the first.

He moved just as cautiously through the gates, the only exit from the courtyard, but here again there was no one laying in wait. The Land Rover was still standing against the kerb, and he decided that they had probably entered Kabul without being marked down. Despite his fears Korovin had not organized as speedily as he had expected. The night was cold and just as he had described, dark, swirling and with practically no visibility. He relaxed a little, for such a night was in his favour.

He left the Land Rover by the kerb,

calculating that he could find his way more easily on foot. He walked briskly and again the exercise was a pleasure. His limbs had been cramped up for too long and he needed the walk. Provided that he kept to the main streets he was confident that he could find his way, and now that he knew that Caroline's apartment was not yet being watched he had no worries that Mannering would be recaptured during his absence.

He found his way back to the Spinzar Hotel, and his thoughts lingered for a moment on the warm luxury of his own centrally heated room. He had not yet officially booked out, although he had informed the management that he would be absent for a few days, but now it did not look as though he would have time to enjoy any more of the hotel's comforts. He kept to the far side of the road as he hurried past, and followed Sharif's directions down to the river.

He was thankful now that he had found the time to familiarize himself with Kabul before the start of the present operation. He found the river with no trouble, and even in the fog he could smell its unsanitary banks as he crossed the bridge. He hurried on and soon came to the wide avenue that divided the older part of the city. He stepped off the pavement and plunged into the fog, losing all landmarks as he crossed the open road. There was no traffic, and although it was not really late Kabul might have been a deserted ghost town. He continued down the road opposite and now he could once again smell smoke in the air, smoke from hidden fires and the kebab stalls that were lost in the cluttered bazaars on either side. There were more people here, strange shrouded and turbanned figures hurrying through the night.

He found the Pamir Hotel on his left. The name showed in feeble lights above the entrance that was reached by three narrow steps. The door was closed, and proved to be stiff and heavy when Larren pushed it open. The Pamir was a poor-class hotel with an ordinary table for a reception desk. Behind the desk was a key rack, a crude pigeon-hole arrangement for letters that was empty, and a large framed portrait of His Majesty Mohammed Zahir Shah, the ruling monarch of Afghanistan. There was a flight of stairs with a faded carpet leading to the upper floor, and Larren hoped that his arrival would pass unseen, then a young Afghani appeared yawning from the far end of the small foyer.

Larren explained that he had a friend in room seventeen. The youth, who was presumably the hotel clerk, seemed a little dubious. His English was limited and he had to scratch his head while Larren explained for the second time. Then he shrugged and indicated that Larren could go up. It was only a brief delay but it was a nuisance. The clerk's English might be bad, but to anyone who spoke his own tongue he would certainly be able to describe Larren's appearance. There was no reason why that should be important, but Larren didn't like it.

He reached the second floor and followed the drab strip of carpet along a dimly lit corridor. Dark faces stared at him curiously from an open bedroom which he walked quickly past, and then he stopped before a door bearing the number 17. A glass panel at the top of the door showed that there was a light inside and he knocked sharply.

There was no answer.

A note of warning began singing in Larren's brain. The sixth sense was instinct and there were faint vibrations tingling the ends of his nerves. He knocked again, but there was no sound from within the room. When he tried the door he found that it was locked.

Larren drew out his wallet as he glanced both ways along the corridor. There was no one in sight and he extracted a thin plastic card. The lock was a simple yale that yielded almost immediately. He returned the card and the wallet to his inside pocket and gently pushed the door open with his left hand. The fingers of his right stayed close to his left sleeve, only inches from the flat hilt of the knife strapped to his arm.

The room appeared to be empty, and after a moment to listen and exercise his other senses, Larren relaxed. He closed the door and surveyed the room.

It was a simple bed-sitting room that showed obvious signs of having been recently disturbed. There was an open door beyond the bed that revealed a small bathroom, and Larren went slowly towards it. His face was cold and bleak even before he looked inside, and his expression did not change as he regarded Gastoni's corpse.

The American lay just inside the bathroom door, dressed only in trousers and a vest. There was still a coating of shaving cream down one side of his dark, craggy jaw and a safety razor had tumbled from his fingers. A broad, hairy chest showed beneath the string vest, but it was very still. The eyes were wide open, staring upwards as though the blank ceiling held some terrible, hypnotic beauty. His throat had been very savagely cut and there was an unnecessary amount of blood. Ray Gastoni had joined his Italian ancestors, and he wasn't going to be a useful man to have around at all.

There was a shaving brush standing on the edge of the washbasin, and there was still a few inches of soapy water in the basin itself. Larren delicately tested the temperature with one finger and found that the water was still warm. The two rooms were empty now, but he had missed Gastoni's killers by a matter of minutes.

He went back into the bedroom and examined the mess. A leather wallet lay on the floor, with a few letters and cards bearing Gastoni's name scattered around it. There was no money and the obvious inference was that Gastoni had been robbed by some ordinary thief. The thief, or thieves, had been surprised by the American appearing from the bathroom, but had been quick enough to cut his throat before he could make any out-cry.

It was all self-explanatory, and for a rushed job it was pretty effective. But Larren knew that Gastoni would never have been taken by any ordinary thief. The hand of Korovin had very clearly pointed the finger and pulled the strings.

Larren guessed that Gastoni must have been known to his opposite numbers amongst the Russians working in Kabul for some time. Ordinarily it would have been a technical mistake to kill him, for then they would have to start all over again on the long task of identifying his replacement. It was rare for an espionage agent to be deliberately killed, it was usually much more profitable to have them watched. The fact that the ultimate step had been taken with Kabul's CIA man meant that the Russians wanted Nevile Mannering's return very badly indeed; so badly that they had eliminated the American in advance to remove the only possible source of aid to Mannering's escape.

Larren disturbed nothing. His nerves were still tingling and he moved only his head as he looked all around the room. There was one window that had probably been the means of exit for the killers. The fact that they had left the light on meant that they had left in a hurry, for the burning light and the lack of response from within had been the first clear indication that something was wrong. No one had passed him in the corridor, and so the window was the obvious answer to the killer's retreat.

He didn't approach the window, for there would be nothing to see and there was no advantage in showing his own face. There was nothing more that he could do here and the tactical move was a fast retreat. He switched off the light and then went back into the corridor, closing and re-locking the door behind him. Someone else would have to say prayers for Ray Gastoni, because Larren had no time.

He left the hotel calmly, showing no signs of hurry, and nodded politely to the clerk at the desk as he went out. The clerk had seen his face once so it was no longer important, it was merely unfortunate that they had met at all.

In the street the fog was still thick, and Larren turned right with every sense again alert. The tingling still continued along his nerves, and he knew exactly why that feeling persisted. If Gastoni's killers had lingered long enough to realize that it was another European and not a member of the hotel staff who had disturbed them, then it was possible that they were still waiting around. They would know the reasons for the killing they had just performed, and they would be intelligent enough to realize that Larren must be one of the men for whom Korovin was searching so urgently.

Strange, turbanned figures, muffled against the cold, lurched past him in the gloom, threatening, half-glimpsed shadows in the night. His muscles tensed and his heart skipped a beat as each one loomed into the close range of his vision but he was not attacked. However, he knew that any attack would not come clumsily from the front, but silently from behind. He walked with every sense alert, relying mostly upon his ears and his instinct, and gradually he knew that he was being followed. He could not explain how or when he had first sensed the presence of his shadows in the fog but he knew that they were there. Being shadowed was no new experience, it had happened many times before, and the knowledge that they were there was part of a deep animal instinct for recognizing an old situation. Larren was an old hand, and civilization was only a partial veneer on a man who had lived much of his life on the level of the jungle.

He wondered grimly whether they would attempt to follow him and locate his base, or whether flushed by their recent success with Gastoni they would close in for another kill.

12

Attempt to Kill

Larren felt that there were two men behind him, but couldn't be sure. However, two was the usual number for a job such as this. His brain shifted on to well-oiled tracks as he calculated the alternatives. He could cut and run, and the odds were good that he could lose his shadows in the fog no matter how well they might know the streets of Kabul. The second alternative was to turn and flush them out, taking the initiative by making the first attacking move.

Those first thoughts were governed by impulse, but were checked by his training and a dose of cold logic. He knew that he was being followed, and if he made the first move then he would throw away that brief advantage. The game had become a duel of wits and there was one fact that he desperately needed to know. He did not think now that Korovin had located Caroline Brand's apartment, but he could not be sure. Gastoni's killers might have found her telephone number or some other betraying sign in the American's hotel room. If that was so then the two men trailing his footsteps would not need to follow him all the way back, they would come in for the kill. The balance of possibilities had shifted and Larren had to know whether his base was still unknown to the enemy. The only sure way to find out was to wait and see what happened.

He reached the broad main avenue and started across, and now he heard definite footsteps behind him. One of his shadows had stepped off the kerb into the road and had unwittingly landed a little less softly than before. The dank, swirling darkness blotted out everything else and Larren did not look round. There was silence behind him again, yet he knew that his shadows were still there, unseen and unheard, like stalking phantoms in the night. Larren had previously walked with his hands deep in the pockets of his overcoat to protect them from the bitter cold, but now he walked like a Chinese with his hands across his chest and hidden in his sleeves. His fingers stayed warm and supple, and close to the comforting hilt of the knife.

They came in as he crossed the bridge over the Kabul River. It was a predictable spot for an attack. They had followed him far enough to ascertain that he was heading in the general direction of Caroline Brand's apartment, and by tumbling his body into the river they could ensure that he would not be discovered until morning. The bridge was deserted as Larren started across, and he knew that it would be now or never. If the attack failed to come then he would have to lose his two shadows before he led them any closer to his base, but the attack came.

He heard the quick rush of footsteps as he reached the crest of the bridge. He wheeled, crouching and drawing the knife from his sleeve. Only by going low did he save himself, for the first man was upon him so swiftly that they collided as he turned. A hostile knife blade slashed above him, missing only by inches, and Larren swung his left shoulder hard into the man's groin. Unable to stop, the would-be killer flew headlong to crash down behind him, and then the second man loomed up out of the night.

Like the first he was a hook-nosed villain dressed in a turban and rags. He came in fast but held back when he saw his companion go sprawling. Larren had straightened up and adopted a defensive stance, the knife held low and a little to the right side of his body, his left arm straight across his chest, the hand flat and stiffened into a second chopping weapon. Larren saw the Afghani hesitate in his approach, and while the man fumbled off-balance he switched deftly from defence to attack. He lunged with the knife. The Afghani countered with his own blade and danced aside, alert for a sweeping blow from that stiffened hand. Instead he caught a driving kick from Larren's right foot squarely between the legs. The baggy Moslem trousers had stopped the toe of Larren's shoe from having its full effect, but even so the man had received a crippling blow. He doubled up and then Larren used his left hand in a chopping blow to the neck, tumbling the man into a heap on the roadway.

If his training had not been so thorough he would have died then, stabbed in the back while he surveyed his victory. But his training had been thorough, he spared no time for self-satisfaction, but wheeled immediately to locate his remaining opponent. The first man had lost his turban when he struck the ground, but he had regained his breath and his feet, and his knife was still gripped fast in his hand.

They were both breathing harshly, and Larren knew that this time there could be no half-measures. This man had taken one hard fall but still he showed no hesitation, and that made him the most dangerous of the two. The Afghani was tall with an arrogant face that was slightly reminiscent of Sharif, another descendant of nomad stock. Larren remembered Sharif's words, after the age of seven an Afghani was immune to everything except a bullet. He hoped that an exception could also be made for a knife.

They circled each other on the fog-shrouded bridge, and the primitive animal that was deep in Larren's soul savoured the moment. Time was meaningless and there had been no progress since the dawn of mankind. They were two hunters and one of them had to die. Man preyed upon man and only the strongest could survive, that was evolution and life's law. The particular stakes of the present conflict became momentarily meaningless.

The Afghani only just beat Larren to the attack. He sprang with all the speed and ferocity of a starving panther, and he was utterly careless of any injury to his free arm as he used it to batter Larren's knife hand to one side. His own blade darted for Larren's groin and almost struck home. Larren twisted back on his left heel, grabbing the Afghani's shoulder with his left hand and continuing to pivot sharply as he hurled the man across the road. The Afghani recovered from the impetuous force of his rush and spun round once more. He dropped into a crouch but he was too late. He had lost the initiative, and Larren followed up with a ruthlessness that matched his own. Larren's left hand came down in a savage chop that struck the defending knife hand away at the wrist, and then he killed. He struck up and underneath the rib cage to the heart.

The Afghani made a spasmodic grunting sound, and then fell back until he was stopped by the wall of the bridge. Larren withdrew his knife, wiped it on the dead man's tattered jacket and then toppled him over the edge. There was a faint splash as he hit the trickle of water that groped its way along the river-bed below, and then silence. Larren turned away, still wary, but the man with the ruptured groin had already chosen to crawl off into the night.

There were sounds in the night, footsteps and voices approaching hesitantly through the fog. The sounds of the scuffle had been heard and it was time for Larren to make himself scarce. He stooped quickly to pick up the knife and the brown cloth turban that had been dropped by his late opponent, and threw them over the bridge to join their owner. Then he sheathed his knife, turned up his collar and hurried away.

* * *

On his return Larren again had to pass the Spinzar Hotel, but again he did not pass close enough to see the travel-stained Dormobile van with the dirt-obscured number plates that was parked close by. However, even if he had seen the van it was doubtful that he would have given it a second thought, for there were too many other problems on his mind. The van still sported its cheerful hand-painted slogans: *The Three MustGetTheirs*, *Which Way Is East?* and *Kabul Or Bust*. The van and its three occupants had arrived in Kabul three days previously. The girl and the young man had amused themselves with a little sight-seeing at the end of their long overland trek, but the older man had been content to relax and wait.

There was still no sign of a watch being kept on Caroline's apartment when Larren returned, but he was not deceived. He felt sure that the apartment must be compromised. The night was still dark and murky, and he was glad to get back into the warm, lighted room where his companions waited. Caroline and Sharif were alert, relaxing only when they saw that he was alone. Mannering came out of the inner bedroom where he had been resting, still pale and nervous, and looking much nearer to sixty than his fifty-two years.

Caroline said quietly:

"Welcome back. But I expected to see Ray with you. Will he co-operate?"

Larren poured himself a dose of medicinal whisky. The *Old Kentucky* bottle was nearly empty, and he had to remind himself that they were now cut off from the source of supply. He said wearily:

"Gastoni isn't going to co-operate with anyone, except perhaps the angels. The

Russians must have known for a long time that he was the top CIA representative in Kabul, and the only man that we could approach for help. They got there before me. When I reached the Pamir Hotel Gastoni was already suffering from a cut throat."

There was a shocked silence. Mannering's face achieved the impossible and turned a shade whiter. Caroline bit down on her lower lip, and the wave of dark gold hair masked her face as she bowed her head and stared down at the carpet. Sharif had drawn himself up like an angry hawk, and after a moment he said harshly:

"You mean that Ray is dead — murdered by the Russians?"

Larren nodded. "I'm sorry. He didn't want to become involved, but they didn't give him a chance to let that be known: They're taking no chances at all."

Sharif's face was bleak. Larren could sense the hot blood rising in the Afghani's veins. The hawk eyes became cruel and vicious, and without another word Sharif picked up his coat and walked towards the door. Larren said quietly:

212

"Where are you going?"

Sharif paused, and then gave him a bitter look.

"Ray was a very close friend of mine, and an Afghani has a rigid code of honour. Blood must pay for blood. I think you are right, Mister Larren, when you suggest that Ray must have been known to our enemies. But there are Soviet agents in Kabul who are also known to me. If they want bloodshed, then by Allah, bloodshed they shall have."

"Relax a minute, you haven't heard the full story." Larren knew that he had to talk fast to prevent the younger man from rushing blindly into a killing spree. Retaliation was a luxury that they could not afford. He went on carefully: "The killers trailed me when I came out of the hotel. They tried to make it a double, but that was a mistake because I knew that they were around. One of them is already dead. I killed him and pushed his body into the Kabul River. The other escaped with a kick in the testicles that's ruined his sex life at least. The score's about

213

even, so there's no reason to go on the rampage."

Sharif said coldly: "You may be satisfied, but Ray was my personal friend."

Larren nodded slowly. "I understand your feelings. You knew him much closer than any of us. But revenge isn't our only problem. The fact that I was attacked means that the Russians must have a very good idea of where we are. Otherwise they would have stayed out of sight and tried to follow me all the way back here. Don't ask me how they located this building. Perhaps they did have a lookout watching the north road and were able to follow us when we entered the city as I first feared. Or, perhaps they found a clue to this address when they killed Gastoni. Either way the signs show that they know where we are, and that means that we have to get Mannering out of here pretty quickly, before they can work out some means of getting him back."

Sharif's face had not relented, and after a pause Larren added frankly: "If you feel that you must indulge in some killing of your own to avenge your personal honour, then I won't stop you. But if you do start off on a campaign of blood for blood, then the odds are that you'll end up spilling some of your own. I don't want that to happen, apart from the fact that we need you here."

The Afghani hesitated, and then Caroline added weight to the argument. She said very quietly:

"Sharif, the job is always more important than the people concerned. That's why we do this kind of job, even though each one of us knows that it could cost his or her life. Ray Gastoni knew that too, and even though he was unfortunate enough to die because of the operations of a rival intelligence service, I still think he would agree that the job must take priority. The present job is to get Mannering back to London, and it would be a shame to leave it half-finished now that we have already achieved so much."

Sharif stared at her, and then at Mannering. His gaze was faintly contemptuous, and it was clear that he considered Mannering as a poor rate of exchange. He was silent for a moment, balancing the subtle qualities of conscience and honour against reason and common-sense. Then slowly he compromised.

"All right, I will stay. But when our mutual business is over, then I shall still have private business to attend."

Larren nodded, although inwardly he hoped that once the heat of the moment had passed he might be able to restrain the impulsive young Afghani from slaughtering every known Communist agent in Afghanistan when the present crisis was over.

"That's fine," he said. "But I'm afraid that once again we are being pretty fiercely pressed by time. We have to move quickly before the other side can close in." He turned to Caroline. "Do you have a map?"

Caroline responded by promptly producing a large-scale map of Afghanistan from a sideboard drawer. They cleared the coffee cups, sandwich plates and whisky glasses away from the table and then spread the map out. Sharif and

Mannering came closer and only Aseli stayed apart. The little man knew that something was wrong, but until Sharif translated more fully he was content to wait and devote his attention to the last beef sandwich.

The map told a simple story. There were only three main routes out of Kabul. The first was north through the Salang Pass to Mazar-i-Sharif, the road that they had already travelled. Then there was the road east, the favourite invasion route and the scene of so many bloody battles, through the Kabul Gorge and the famous Khyher Pass to Peshawar in Pakistan. Finally the south road to Khandahar.

Sharif said grimly: "The Khyber Pass is probably our best route. It takes us to the closest frontier. But for the same reasons it is the route that our friend Korovin will expect us to take, and it is a dangerous road. A car has to pass above many steep precipices while going through the Kabul Gorge. It is an ideal place for another car to run us off the road and send us crashing to our deaths.

And we must remember that now that Mannering has betrayed the Russians, Korovin will perhaps be as happy to see him dead as to take him back."

Mannering said nothing, but closed his eyes as though he could already see his grave.

Caroline said thoughtfully: "What about Khandahar? It's three hundred miles south, but it's a perfect road and we could drive there through the night. From there we can again strike across the Pakinstan frontier to Quetta."

Mannering opened his eyes. A thought had just struck him and he looked suddenly hopeful. He said nervously:

"Couldn't you just take me to the British Embassy here in Kabul? There I should be safe until all the fuss dies down."

Larren did not enjoy crushing the man's hopes, but he had no choice, and Mannering's face faltered back to normal again as he answered.

"I'm sorry, but there isn't any point. Smith wants you in London, so we'll still have to get you out of the Embassy again, and out of Afghanistan. The British Ambassador here won't thank us for embarrassing him with your company, and in any case, tonight while this fog helps to shield our movements is still our best hope of getting you out."

They turned to the map again, and considered Caroline's last suggestion, while Mannering turned away and sat down with his head in his hands.

"Whichever way we go I think Korovin will have the roads watched," Sharif said dubiously. "We could turn off into the mountains of the Kohi Baba from the north or south roads, but he knows that we have only the three initial choices for getting out of Kabul."

"Four," Larren mused. "There's a minor little road here that follows the valley of the Logar River, running south and then joining the Khandahar road at Ghazni." He thought hard and then looked at Caroline. "Do you have a car?"

She nodded. "It's a natural precaution. There's a few hire cars available for tourists, and I was able to get hold of a Russian Moskvitch saloon. There's no garage here so I have to keep it a couple of streets away."

Larren smiled. "It couldn't be better. If you can get out to that car unseen, fill it up with petrol and then drive a few miles down the Logar Valley and wait for us. We'll give you half an hour's start and then follow with Mannering in the Land Rover. We'll rendezvous with you, make a quick changeover of vehicles, and then double back into Kabul and out again on the main road south to Khandahar. We're assuming the worst — that they will be watching all roads and that they do know that we're driving a Land Rover. With luck we'll have them chasing their tails up the Logar Valley, thoroughly convinced that we haven't had the nerve to use the main roads."

His confidence was not fully shared by the other members of the party, but none of them could make any suitable alternatives. Mannering got up to take another look at the map, and then turned away again and shakily poured himself another whisky while the details were discussed. Caroline was reasonably sure that she could leave through the back of the building without being seen, and finally she returned Larren's gun before she pulled on a thickly-fleeced sheepskin overcoat, one of the native products of Kabul. Larren tried to refuse the gun but she was severely practical.

"Don't argue, Simon. Mannering is the only one of us who is important, and now that you're resuming your position as his bodyguard you're the one who might need the firepower."

Larren hesitated, and then Sharif interrupted.

"I do not think that you should go out there alone and unarmed. This is no job for a woman. Give me your keys and I will take your place."

Caroline smiled. "That's a sweet offer, but really I'm not an ordinary sort of woman, and Whitehall expects me to earn my keep. Besides, you might not be able to find the car, it's in a rather secluded yard."

Her smile included them all, and Larren thought that the coat suited her well. It was a dark green suede with hand-embroidered patterns of flowers stitched on with lighter green thread. She buttoned it up and smiled again in parting, and then she went out through the back kitchen and a staircase that led down into the interior of the building. Larren watched her go, weighed the Smith & Wesson in his palm, and hoped that she would encounter no dangers.

Mannering said hesitantly: "Why can't we go with her now? Why can't we all go out together to the other car?"

"Because if the back way out is being watched then you would be recognized and that would be the finish," Larren explained wearily. "Alone there's a good chance that Caroline can slip through, and then we are in a position to switch cars outside Kabul and so swing the odds into our favour."

Mannering licked his lips but again fell into a bitter silence. He was unhappy and unconvinced, but he was wholly in their hands and he knew it. Sharif was also on edge, but for different reasons, the Afghani still bore a striking resemblance to a caged hawk. Only Larren was outwardly calm. They had given Caroline half an hour, and they waited.

13

South to Khandahar

It was not an easy thirty minutes. Caroline Brand was a very capable young woman, as Larren well knew, but she was still a woman. Her training would enable her to deal very swiftly and effectively with any ordinary attacker, but she would still be at a disadvantage with an equally well-trained man, and Larren had to remember that it was possible that Korovin himself was somewhere outside in the darkness. For some unknown reason he began to recall the occasions when he had made love to her in the past, and there was a strange feeling of disturbance in his stomach. He wished then that he had made her keep the Smith & Wesson.

However, it was too late now and they could only wait. There was no way of knowing whether she had accomplished her task or not, and that was the worst part. They could only wait until the specified time limit was up, and then act on the hopeful assumption that nothing had gone wrong.

Sharif bore the waiting badly, still showing his frustration in his desire to exact an immediate vengeance on behalf of Gastoni. Also his college education in the United States had given him a veneer of American gallantry that irked him for sitting still and allowing a woman to take risks. Larren watched the Afghani's brooding face, and inwardly he was worried. Sharif had been invaluable, and both he and Mannering owed him their lives, but he was young and reckless and the continuing pressure was making him impatient. His nerve and his stamina seemed everlasting, but his self-control was a different matter. Larren knew that if the pressure increased then Sharif would have to be watched to prevent any hot-headed action that might precipitate disaster.

It was a relief to move when the thirty minutes were up. They pulled on their overcoats, and Sharif exchanged a few low, last-minute words with Asefi to ensure that the little man understood exactly what was happening. Larren eased the safety catch off the Smith & Wesson, and then switched off the light. They moved to the door and Mannering's voice whispered nervously in the darkness.

"Why can't we go out the back way and follow your friend? It'll be safer."

Larren said grimly: "Because we still have to come back to the front of the building to pick up the Land Rover. And in any case it suits our plans to have them see us drive off. There are four of us, and the other side won't know that I'm the only one that is armed, so I don't think they'll try to stop us driving away. They won't risk a pitched gun battle in the middle of the city. They'll want things done more quietly or at least in a lonelier spot."

Mannering became silent again, and they opened the door and filed out on to the balcony. Sharif gripped Mannering's arm, a little harder than was necessary and Larren led the way down into the courtyard. They were all tense and alert, but if there was a cordon of watching eyes no one moved to stop them. They moved in a close group towards the gates, and Larren was disturbed to see that the fog was clearing. The range of visibility had extended and he cursed softly. It seemed as though Korovin, or some fate especially kind to him, was actually controlling the elements. Larren's luck had changed right from the moment that Korovin had appeared in the background of the scene.

Larren stopped the party as they passed through the open gates to quit the courtyard. Asefi went forward alone to check that the Land Rover was undisturbed and Larren covered him with the Smith & Wesson. The little man climbed into the cab, glanced into the back to verify that it was empty, and then started the engine. Larren had half expected to find the engine sabotaged and felt another spasm of relief as he heard it roar.

They moved in a rush now, Sharif and Mannering scrambling into the back of the Land Rover while Larren joined Asefi in the front. The little man gunned the engine and they leaped away. No one jumped in front of them. There were no shouts, no shots, no explosions, and Larren began to wonder again whether he was overestimating Korovin and taking too many precautions.

With the aid of the headlights they could see almost clearly now. The fog still lay in grey patches, but it was definitely disappearing. Mannering had noticed it too and he tugged at Larren's shoulder to attract his attention.

"Larren, the fog is almost gone. Why don't we go straight to the airport? We can fly out as you originally planned."

Larren twisted round to face him and he was becoming angry. Mannering was too scared and he didn't stop to think. Larren said:

"Because our flight will stay cancelled until morning. All the normal passengers will have been sent back to their hotels by now, and the airline won't risk a take-off until the fog is completely cleared. We are the only ones with any special hurry to get out of Kabul."

Mannering fell silent again, biting down his disappointment, but Sharif said curtly:

"There is a car following us. It appeared immediately after we left Miss Brand's apartment."

Larren swore softly and looked behind. Mannering had distracted him and he realized that he should have expected this. The twin yellow headlights of the trailing car were unmistakable, and now he knew why they had been allowed to leave the apartment, and why the Land Rover had not been touched. The other side were hoping to catch up with him outside the city where they could close in without any fear of interruptions. He felt a brief sense of satisfaction at knowing that he had been right in thinking that the apartment was under observation, but it was short-lived and one that he would have been happy to do without. He said grimly:

"Can we lose them?"

Sharif translated to Asefi and the little man looked dubious. He hunched over the wheel and then put his foot hard down. The Land Rover accelerated and shot forward. Larren leaned out of the window and looked behind. The following headlights retreated, then steadied as the driver of the second car accelerated in turn, and then gradually the gap began to close again. The driver of the tail car was equally as competent as Asefi and probably even more familiar with the streets of Kabul.

They were racing down the wide, maple-lined avenue that ran past the Royal Palace to the Spinzar Hotel, although the buildings on either side were still shrouded by the remains of the fog. Larren rapped more orders for Sharif to translate, and Asefi swung the Land Rover round a sharp bend to the right. It was the opposite direction to the way they wanted to go, but now they could not escape from the city until they had shaken off the pursuing car. To the best of Larren's knowledge Asefi no longer had a wad of chewing gum in his mouth, but nonetheless his jaws still moved in absent-minded chewing movements as he concentrated hard on the road ahead.

They zig-zagged frantically, twisting and turning through the streets of Kabul with their tyres howling in protest on every corner. Twice they all but killed luckless pedestrians unfortunate enough to attempt to cross the road in their path, and on the second occasion they actually tumbled an old man into the gutter as they roared past. He appeared before them like a ragged old prophet, hypnotized by the spell of their lights. Larren could almost count the wrinkles in the lined brown forehead beneath his turban, and was almost hypnotized in turn by the horrified stare of the watery eyes. Then Asefi swerved desperately in the last moment, and it was the rush of movement rather than a blow from the car itself that knocked the old man aside. Larren glimpsed his mouth, open in a scream like a stump-filled gap almost obscured by whiskers, and then the old man was rolling aside. Larren looked back and saw him struggling to rise, and was relieved when the car behind them managed to miss him in turn by a wider margin.

Asefi was shaken by the incident, and his foot slackened slightly on the accelerator pedal. On the last three bends he had all but overturned the Land Rover, but the thought that he might have killed the innocent old Afghani had upset him more than the prospect that he might kill them all, including himself. However, Larren did not try to force him into further speed. There was still enough of the fog lingering to constitute a driving hazard, and Asefi was handicapped by the fact that he had to search ahead and find his way. The pursuing car had the Land Rover's tail light as a guide, and had the advantage of a split-second warning every time that a turning was made. They had failed to shake off the second car, but Larren had already decided upon an alternative to any further suicidal driving. He said quietly:

"Sharif, tell Asefi to take the next corner that comes up, and then slam his brakes on and stop immediately that we get round. I'll do the rest from there."

Sharif hesitated, but refrained from asking questions and gave the necessary instructions. Asefi glanced doubtfully at Larren, and received an unsmiling nod to confirm the order. The little man pouted dubiously and then looked back at the road.

The following car was fifty yards behind when the next corner came up. Asefi took it fast in a tight, screaming turn, and then did exactly as he had been told and applied the brakes. The Land Rover screeched to a stop, but the wheels were still turning as Larren pushed open his side door and jumped down on to the road. The Land Rover carried on past him as he crouched on one knee. He raised his left arm at eye level to provide a steady bar across his face, and firmly rested the Smith & Wesson .38 across his left wrist.

There was another scream of tyres, and then headlights came flashing round the corner and driving straight at him. He steadied the automatic, squinting above it and pumping off four fast shots. The hand gun was not accurate at a distance, but the distance was narrowing fast and the car made a big target. The first bullet zeroed down the headlight beam to end in a smash of glass, and then Larren slightly lowered aim. Either the third or fourth shot burst the off-side tyre and the car went careering across the road out of control. It was a big black saloon with several men inside, but they had all been startled by the attack. The car crashed in a nightmare of explosive sound against the far wall, but Larren was already up and running to catch up with the Land Rover. He grabbed for the door and hauled himself in, and Asefi needed no urging to get under way. They were gone and out of range before a return shot could be fired.

After a pause while Larren replaced the safety on the automatic and slipped it into his pocket, Sharif said admiringly:

"That was excellent, we should have done it before."

Mannering said nothing, and Larren guessed that his face would be pale and sick as usual. Asefi made a vague puffing sound with his cheeks that could have meant anything and carried on driving.

They had driven in circles around the northern part of the city, but now they found their way back to the centre. They crossed the Kabul River by the same bridge where Larren had recently been obliged to fight for his life, continued to the main avenue through the bazaars and there turned left. Soon they were leaving the city behind and following the road out to the Logar valley. Larren was no longer certain that the exit roads would be watched, for Korovin might have reasoned that the shadowing car would be enough to keep track of their movements. However, they could afford to take no chances, they definitely needed to make the changeover of vehicles, and they could hardly leave Caroline stranded while they took a different route, and so they stuck to their original plans.

There was still enough fog to limit the power of their headlights, and in the darkness they could see very little but the road itself as they left Kabul. Caroline had arranged to wait six miles outside the city, and as the sixth mile moved up on the speedometer clock Larren was relieved to see her muffled figure waving them down from the roadside. The dark green sheepskin coat made her easy to identify, and Asefi stopped the Land Rover as they drew level. Caroline put her head inside the open window and said breathlessly:

"You're late. I was afraid that something had happened."

"Something did," Larren said. "But I'll tell you all about it later. Where's the car?"

"Over here."

She pulled her head back again and vanished round the front of the Land Rover, for Asefi had already switched off the double beam of the headlights. Larren got down and followed her, and Sharif and Mannering came to join him. The hired Moskvitch saloon was pulled up off the far side of the road, and already pointed back to Kabul in readiness for the return trip. It was a smaller and more handsome car than the bulky Volga that they had driven from Samarkand, and Larren had to admit that the Russian factories occasionally turned out a smartly styled vehicle. Caroline took her seat behind the wheel and Mannering was pushed hurriedly into the back. Sharif and Larren returned for a final word with Asefi.

They were reluctant to part from the faithful little man who had served them so well, but the Moskvitch saloon could only carry four in comfort, and already they had decided that it would not be wise to abandon the Land Rover where it might be swiftly found. Instead Asefi was to drive on down the Logar valley until he found a town or village where he could simply stay out of sight for a few days. Then he would return the Land Rover to the construction company's yard in Kabul, and go back to his own normal routine.

They said their farewells, shook hands firmly, and as a parting gesture Larren ensured that Asefi had enough money to enjoy his period of idleness. Then the Land Rover drove off into the night with Asefi waving cheerfully as he vanished into the darkness, while Larren and Sharif wasted no time in getting into their waiting car.

Larren joined Caroline in the front, while Sharif took the back seat beside Mannering. Caroline started the car and as they drove back to Kabul Larren explained why their rendezvous had been delayed. Caroline listened with set lips, and then said:

"You were lucky that the following car had to use headlights, otherwise they might have followed you without being seen, and then we would all have been caught nicely in the open while you changed over from the Land Rover."

"They had no choice," Larren said thankfully. "Asefi was driving too fast, and at that speed there was still enough fog to make blind driving dangerous."

Caroline nodded, for the fog was thickening up again and she could see why headlights were a necessity. A slow car might have been trailed through the fog without using lights, but not a fast one. She drove until they were about to enter Kabul again and then said:

"Your late friends must have realized

that there were four people in the Land Rover. Now there are four people in this car and if we are seen they might decide that the number isn't a coincidence. I think Sharif and Mannering should get down on the floor while we pass through the city and stay out of sight. There are a couple of travelling rugs that they can use to cover themselves."

Sharif grumbled, but finally complied, and he and Mannering got down on to the floor. Larren leaned back to arrange the rugs over their heads, and then faced the front again as they re-entered the city streets. Larren didn't turn up his coat collar because that was too old-fashioned and obvious. Instead he turned his head to face into the car, as though he was watching or talking to Caroline. He wasn't sure whether his face could be recognized, but this way any chance light from outside would only fall on the side or the back of his head.

Caroline drove calmly back to the river, following its course through the narrow gap between the two hulking shoulders of mountain that squeezed Kabul in the middle. Here she crossed the river and drove on to the main road south to Khandahar. If there was a lookout stationed on the way out of Kabul then he was well hidden, for there was nothing to alarm them. They left the city behind and Caroline was able to put her foot down and speed up their progress. They had a filthy night, but it was a good road, comparable to any in Europe, and they expected to reach Khandahar by dawn.

14

Ambush

Larren was able to relax as they followed the smooth road south, but he couldn't sleep. Even though he was tired his mind was still active. For the moment it seemed that they had a chance, but he had already received too many painful lessons on the folly of counting his chickens before they were hatched. He knew that the KGB spy network extended throughout Afghanistan, so if Korovin did anticipate their intentions there was no need for him to follow and deal with them personally. Korovin could operate from remote control. Larren remembered the dark, cruel face that he had seen but once, and he remembered the details of the man's ruthlessly successful career that were filed away in the fat dossier in Smith's Whitehall office. Korovin was a lethal opponent, and in all probability the

241

best man in the ranks of the KGB. Larren had once before met a man whom he had considered his own equal, a Greek named Christos whom he had killed on an island in the Aegean.[1] He had almost lost to Christos in their final duel, and Christos had not had the full weight of the KGB behind him. Korovin, Larren sensed, was a man of that same calibre, and he did have that extra weight. Also Korovin was operating close to his own home territory, while Larren was all but isolated in a strange land. Larren's thoughts were gloomy, and he would have given a lot to know exactly where Korovin was at this very moment, how much the man knew, and, more than anything else, what was he thinking and planning.

At the wheel Caroline had settled down for the long drive through the night. For her the flight was just beginning and she was both rested and fresh. She was also a fast and capable driver, for her

---

[1] See Mission of Murder

training had fitted her to handle almost any situation, and so Larren was content to leave the car in her hands. For a few minutes he watched her face, which was faintly visible in the dim light from the control panel. The blue eyes and the frame of dark gold hair made it a beautiful face, but there was strength of character there too. She was a very rare breed of woman, and he suddenly knew that he wanted her very badly. He wondered then if he could persuade her to make love with him again when this present job was over. The reaction of getting out alive, if they did both get out alive, might be enough to weaken her resistance. After all, she wanted him too, or she had before. She had proved to him that her sex drives were normal, and although they both knew that there could be nothing lasting they could live for the moment. It would not be a new compromise.

She sensed his interest and gave him a curious glance, wondering, or perhaps knowing what he was thinking. Larren smiled vaguely and then looked to the road. Behind him Sharif and Mannering were sitting upright, both awake, and again his thoughts took up their wandering. This time around the subject of Mannering.

He was still somewhat dubious about the man whom he had rescued from inside Russia. As yet there had been no time to talk, to ask questions, or to try and feel his way around to Mannering's true beliefs and character. Ever since Samarkand they had been in flight, concentrating on their efforts to escape and keep moving. The nearest opportunity they had had to relax had been on the last two days of driving down to Kabul when they had had Asefi to relieve them at the wheel of the Land Rover, but then Mannering had been too weak from the frontier crossing and had laid only semi-conscious in the back. Now he was much better, but in front of Sharif, Larren was reluctant to ask any probing questions. The Afghani's reaction might well cause another crisis if he were to realize that Larren harboured doubts about Mannering's true value.

Larren wanted to ask exactly what had happened during Mannering's three years inside Russia, and exactly what kind of information he was bringing out to Smith. There were a vast number of questions that he wanted to ask and have answered, but he had to wait for a more favourable time before he could start nailing the man down with any lengthy cross-examination.

Larren glanced back once, but no one spoke to him. Sharif was sitting with his arms folded across his chest, his face brooding in the black shadow of his turban. There were dark thoughts of retribution fermenting in his mind, and Larren guessed that when he returned to Kabul, then someone would have to pay the price for Ray Gastoni. Sharif was an open book, but Mannering was more difficult to read. The ex-diplomat sat in the opposite corner of the back seat, and his stodgy face was grey and tensely drawn in the darkness. There was fear in his mind, but what else? His inner thoughts were hidden and only the fear registered on the surface.

Larren turned away again and watched the road speeding past. A perfect, modern road built by American aid because the Russians had built a similar road on the other side of Afghanistan from Khandahar to Herat, and the Americans had to keep pace. Or was it the other way round, and the Americans had built first only to have the Russians hastening to keep in step. It was not important. Perhaps he was even confused as to whose aid had built which road, but it did not really matter. He was only interested in the fact that the road was there, and that it was speeding their escape.

The miles hurried by. Somewhere on their right were the mountain ranges of the Kohi Baba, the wild interior of Afghanistan, but they saw nothing in the night. After two hours they passed by the large town of Ghazni, and from here the last of the fog cleared. They could see stars now in the freezing black canopy of the sky, and their headlights threw a bright, clear beam down the inky black ribbon of the road. Caroline showed no signs of tiring so Larren dozed. When he awoke another two hours had passed and they had covered over half of their all-night journey. He made Caroline stop and relieved her at the wheel.

The little Moskvitch saloon handled well, although it was not as large and powerful as he would have liked. He decided that he preferred the Volga that they had driven down from Samarkand, despite the other car's clumsy and less stylish appearance. Outside the night was cold and bitter, but in the car the warmth from the heater made them drowsy. His companions dozed again, and Larren was left to contend with his thoughts and the car. The miles and the minutes sped past in company, but after another hour Caroline opened her eyes and demanded the return of the wheel. Larren slowed to a stop and again they changed places.

Caroline drove the rest of the way into Khandahar, but Larren did not sleep again. He rested his eyes for a few minutes, but the night was filtering away and dawn was stealing out of the harsh, bare hills to take its place. He watched the shadows retreat across the yellow-brown desert landscape, and fade into the stark and distant ridges of red and purple rock. Afghanistan provided a fierce variety of colour for such a barren land.

During the drive they had been stopped several times by Afghani soldiers manning small red and white sentry boxes at the roadside, for the road was a toll road and there were charges at various intervals. None of them had liked these brief enforced halts, even though they were routine and the charges were nominal. What disturbed them was that their progress had been recorded and could be traced, and as they approached Khandahar the tension began to build up around them again. They were all awake now that it was daylight, and if Korovin had managed to get a lead on their movements, then they knew that they could expect another attempt to stop their escape as they neared Afghanistan's second largest city. A telephone call could have raced ahead of them, and a reception committee was at least a possibility. Very soon they would know for a fact whether they had succeeded in fooling their enemies, or whether they had failed.

★ ★ ★

The left turn to the second major frontier crossing into Pakistan and the city of Quetta beyond appeared before they entered Khandahar. They turned on to the new road, bringing the slowly rising sun more squarely on their left flank. The range of distant purple mountains was on fire with the sun's rays but they barely noticed its hostile beauty.

The frontier was still fifty miles distant, and so the next hour would prove crucial. If their escape had not been foiled by then they would be safely across the border into Pakistan. As with India there were no advance visas necessary for holders of British passports, so they expected no trouble on the Pakistani side. It had already been agreed that Sharif would take the car back to Kabul, while Larren, Caroline and Mannering would catch a local bus into Quetta. Here there was a small internal airport where they could hope to catch a flight to Karachi on the BOAC air routes. However, these plans depended upon getting through the Afghani side of the frontier.

Their fuel tank was registering empty, and they had to stop while Larren got out and poured in four gallons from the spare petrol can in the boot. Then they continued again, still with Caroline at the wheel. Their nerves were all becoming strained and so she drove fast, anxious to get out of Afghanistan before anything went wrong. There was desert landscape on either side with no threat of danger, and then far ahead they saw a vague obstruction on the road, its outline blurred by the faint heat haze.

As they drew closer the obstruction materialized into one of the large, brightly painted lorries so familiar to Afghan roads. It had apparently broken down and was blocking most of the road. Some four or five men in the usual ragged clothes and large turbans were busily engaged in changing one of the heavy back wheels. The lorry's bonnet had slewed towards the middle of the road, and as she slackened speed to circle round it Caroline said slowly:

"It looks like they've had a blowout."

Larren was not so sure. It was his nature to be suspicious, and at this stage he was prepared to be suspicious of anything. The Afghanis clustered around the tail end of the lorry had stopped work and were standing aside to let the approaching car pass. They were all staring, but there was more than just curiosity in their eyes, their stares were too direct. Then two different facts registered with Larren in the same moment. He sensed Mannering leaning forward behind him to see what was happening, and he knew which face the watching men were searching for. He also noticed the hard bulges under the ragged clothing, and saw the first of the brown hands straying inside a jacket to where one of those bulges was more prominent.

"It's a trap!"

Larren barked the warning and grabbed at the wheel. He pulled hard and the car swung round in a fast turn, cutting past the back of the lorry and shooting off the road into the desert. Caroline was alert enough to slam her foot hard down and the vehicle bounced violently, throwing them all painfully about the interior. Like a team of conjurors working the same synchronized trick the band of men grouped about the lorry had all produced automatics or machine pistols from under their clothes and began firing madly. The car was already halfway past the lorry and Larren would have circled it and returned to the road and a continued flight towards Quetta, and then just in time he saw the double lengths of long spiked chain that had been strung across the hard stony ground to forestall such a move.

The spikes would have burst their tyres and that would have meant their finish. They would have been helpless as the ambush party closed in. Larren swore savagely and continued to wrench hard at the wheel, hauling the car right round in a tight, screaming circle to face back the way they had come. Dirt and stones showered upwards in the process, and for one awful moment Larren thought that he must have shredded the two offside tyres on the spikes. However, there was no pistol-shot burst of an exploding tyre, and despite the rude and excruciating treatment that the car had suffered they kept going. Larren saw that the spiked chains extended as far as the broken terrain of jumbled rock which started some thirty yards from the roadside, so there was no gap through which they could safely take the car. He guessed that there must be similar barriers on the far side of the lorry and they had no choice but to go back.

The men from the lorry were running towards them now, still blazing away with their firearms. The air was hideous with the noise of bullets and several shots ricocheted wildly off the bodywork of the car. Another smashed through the rear window and showered the whole of the back seat with splintering fragments of flying glass. Sharif and Mannering had both ducked low, but Mannering was a fraction too slow and he gave a shrill yelp of pain as blood began to spill quickly from a sharp gash across his face.

Mercifully the ambush party were too hasty and far from accurate. One or two cool shots amongst them would have told a very different story, but they were shooting like cowboys letting off steam and they failed to stop the car. Caroline kept her foot flat down on the floorboards and swaying crazily they raced away. Another fusillade of gunfire blazed hopefully after them, and they heard more bullets skidding off the sides of the once-stylish Moskvitch saloon. Then they were clear. Caroline jolted the car back on to the road and they headed back towards Khandahar.

The nightmare stopped, and the road block and the running men grew smaller and more distant behind them. Soon they faded back into the heat haze and disappeared.

The four faces in the retreating car showed a variety of emotion. Sharif was thunderous with anger. Caroline white and tense. Mannering bleeding and afraid. Only Larren's face showed nothing definite. He tried to think instead. They had failed to get through to Quetta. It would be pointless to try and return to Kabul. And he simply did not know which way to turn next.

15

Trapped

For several miles not one of them spoke. In the back seat Mannering had pulled out a large white handkerchief and was holding it close to the ugly red wound that had appeared along the bone of his right cheek. Beside him Sharif was picking the pieces of broken glass from the seat and his clothing and hurling them with savage disgust through the jagged hole where the rear window had been. Caroline was able to relieve some of her own tension by concentrating on her driving, and by the time they had neared the main road again her face had regained some of its former colour. She saw the road junction coming up and looked to Larren for directions.

"Left," Larren said wearily. "Kabul is no good to us, and there is no other way."

Caroline nodded, slowed the car and turned to the left. Khandahar was directly in front of them, an old city, as old and historic as Kabul but with fewer modern buildings. Many of its walls and buildings were still made of timber and mud. The people were wild-looking, and the traffic consisted mostly of pony traps, donkeys and camels. There were dark cubby-hole shops, and sinister alleyways leading into the mazes behind the main streets. Caroline drove very slowly with no definite purpose, and glanced repeatedly at Larren.

Mannering found his voice first. The last remnants of his nerve were fading, and again Larren was reminded that he was mentally a broken man. Several times his throat had worked without any words being uttered, and when the words did break out they blurted almost hysterically.

"Where are we going? There's nothing here in Khandahar. We can't go back to Kabul, and we can't get into Pakistan. We're trapped in this bloody country." He gripped the back of Caroline's seat and pulled himself forward, his hysteria becoming starkly accusing. "Larren, this is all your fault. Why couldn't you have left me in Samarkand? I didn't even want to be bloody-well rescued. Now you've got us all into a mess and there's no way out."

"Shut up!" Larren said coldly, making two separate words.

Mannering quivered with either rage or humiliation.

"I will not shut up! I'm not just a tame pet to be dragged around as you think fit. I want to know where we're going now? What are you going to do?"

Larren turned slowly in his seat. He said nothing, but the savage message in those grey-green eyes was enough. He had lost patience and Mannering knew it. Mannering chose to shut up.

Sharif watched Mannering subside with contemptuous eyes, then he looked at Larren.

"There is an airport here at Khandahar. Perhaps it is worth a try?"

Larren hesitated, and then shook his head. "No, it's no good. Somehow

Korovin has traced us this far. The road block proves that. He's pretty sure to have the airport guarded as well, and in any case it's only an internal airport, we could only hope to fly to another part of Afghanistan. The KGB is a well-organized and extensive network, and we must have every Russian agent in the country on the lookout for our faces. Our only hope is to get across the frontier."

Caroline was allowing the car to dawdle as she threaded her way through the streets. She had to stop while a string of three heavily-laden camels made their ponderous way across the road in front of their bonnet, and while they waited she asked:

"How do you think Korovin managed to trace us?"

Larren shrugged. "Perhaps Asefi came to grief, but I'm hoping it isn't that. It's more likely that we were betrayed by one of those toll points where we had to pull up on the main road. There isn't a lot of private road traffic in Afghanistan, so we can't help being noticeable, especially by driving overnight. Korovin must have calculated the possibility that we would change cars and put out an enquiry for any car carrying four people, plus a detailed description of Mannering. Those jokers at the road block didn't start reaching for their hardware until they saw Mannering's face."

Caroline twisted her face into an expression of distaste and observed: .

"So we can assume that Korovin, or at least the KGB, have enough influence to make enquiries through those toll checkpoints, and that they telephoned through to Khandahar to have us stopped. That's a lot of influence. It doesn't seem to hold out much hope for the future."

"There is no hope for the future," Mannering said bitterly. "Larren is lost. He doesn't know what to do next. We're all lost."

Larren swung round again, but in the same moment Caroline started the car and circled round the rump of the last slow camel. As she changed into higher gear she said:

"He's right about one thing, Simon.

We have to make a decision. Are we stopping in Khandahar, or driving right through?"

Larren hesitated again, and then said flatly: "Drive straight through. Keep going hard and we'll carry on all the way to Herat. From there we'll make a try at getting into Persia. Korovin knows that Pakistan would be our first choice because it's part of the Commonwealth and for us there are no visa restrictions. If we double north again we might fool him yet."

Sharif said bleakly: "I presume you realize that Herat is another three hundred miles to the north on the western side of Afghanistan. It is another brand-new toll road so there will be more checkpoints to betray our movements. Also the men who staged the road block with the lorry will be able to inform Korovin that we are, to be precise, three men and a woman and that we are driving a black Moskvitch saloon car instead of a Land Rover."

"He's right," Mannering said in anguish. "You're simply driving me round and round Afghanistan in circles, and when we reach Herat we'll find that another telephone call has gone ahead and that we're running into another road block."

Larren felt the rise of exasperation. He knew that Mannering was right and that he was simply formulating desperation plans that had to be altered or discarded as they went along. Every move he made was being foiled but he had to keep trying. He said harshly:

"All right, so we won't drive into Herat. We'll ditch the car before we get there. And we won't be caught in another ambush like that lorry trick. We know what to expect and we'll be prepared in advance. It would be a waste of their time to pull the same routine twice."

He turned fully round in his seat and went on without a pause.

"Sharif, you managed to hire horses for us when we approached the frontier with Russia. Do you think you could find another band of nomads somewhere in the region of Herat. If we could hire more horses then we can avoid the city and trek across country into Persia."

"It might be possible." Sharif sounded dubious.

"It will have to be possible." Larren made a grim smile that was intended to put everyone at their ease, and then turned to face the front. They were leaving Khandahar and there was another long, wearying drive across open road ahead of them.

From behind Mannering asked weakly:

"What happens if we do cross into Persia? We'll be no better off."

"We will if the KGB are still hunting for us in Afghanistan." Larren's temper had relaxed now that their progress had once again acquired purpose, however vague, and so he was less curt. "If we get into Persia unseen there'll be nobody looking out to stop us. We'll make for Tehran and there we will have to take the risk of embarrassing the British Embassy. We can wait there until the necessary entry visas are forged on to our passports, and when they read as though we've entered legally then we can exit legally, and get that long-awaited plane to London."

Caroline glanced up from the wheel and said:

"Simon, you make it all sound so beautifully simple." And then her lips formed a faint smile as she added regretfully: "I only wish that you hadn't made things sound just as simple in Kabul."

There was no answer to that and Larren remained silent.

★ ★ ★

The drive was now developing into a marathon, and they were all desperately tired. Larren, Sharif and Mannering had been on the move almost continuously since they had left Samarkand, and now even Caroline had lost the fresh strength that she had brought to the party at Kabul. She was tired from the long night drive and finally had to relinquish the wheel. She insisted on getting into the back of the car to give some proper attention to Mannering's cut cheek, and so Sharif took over the task of driving. There was a small first-aid box in the car, and they heard Mannering gasp and wince as Caroline cleaned his shallow wound and then taped a pad of medicated lint into position to keep it clean.

When the job was done Caroline tried to sleep, but as with the others before her she found that there was no real comfort in a fast-moving car, and she could only doze. Mannering sat miserably beside her, nursing his hurt and his fears.

Larren tried to look complacent and relaxed, but his outward appearance did not match up with the way he felt. There was something soul-destroying in the fact that they had been forced to turn north again, although they were more accurately heading north-west. The main roads of Afghanistan lay around the mountainous interior like a necklace, with Khandahar dangling like the pendulant jewel. They had come down from the north-east, and now they were circling up and around the central mountains. If they continued past Herat the main road would veer east again towards Mazar-i-Sharif, and then they would have completed the round trip. As Mannering had so wretchedly pointed out, they were going round in circles.

Mannering's condition was now becoming a source of worry, and not only his mental condition. Even if they were able to ditch the car and then find another group of nomads who could be bribed to help them they would still have to face long hours on horseback over some very rough country before they could hope to cross the frontier. They were none of them at their physical best, Mannering least of all, and a rigorous trek might go beyond their capabilities. However, Larren could think of no alternative, and obviously the others were equally at a loss. To find horses and get away from the roads seemed to be their only hope.

The road was another straight, smooth, flat surface along which they could comfortably cruise at the car's top speed. On either side the landscape was of red hills and long flat plains, with dark mountains filling the far distance. They passed very little traffic, a few lorries, an occasional camel or pushbike, and one over-crowded bus. The only signs of life were a few tents, and at intervals a small mud village as old as time. At one of the larger villages they stopped to fill up with petrol and to make a hurried attack on their own hunger and thirst, but they resumed their journey as swiftly as possible.

Larren saw the first of the small red and white toll boxes appearing ahead and swore. They had to slow down and pay the necessary tax, and then they were given a receipt and waved on by a cheerful Afghani soldier. Sharif glanced at Larren's face as he accelerated away and shrugged his shoulders. They could only hope that Korovin's range of influence did not extend so effectively along this more distant stretch of road. Sharif had become unexpectedly fatalistic, and his expression said that their fate was in the hands of Allah.

Throughout the day they drove, and again the miles fell away behind them with the hours. Sharif and Larren alternated at the wheel as they had done on the road down from Samarkand, and so the car was forced to give of its best.

By mid-afternoon they had covered three parts of the three-hundred-and-fifty-mile journey, and the feeling had settled over them that they were doomed to drive on and on through the bare hills and desert for eternity. Then another toll booth appeared ahead.

Larren was at the wheel and reluctantly he slowed the car. There was the usual group of soldiers gossiping around the red and white sentry box, and there was a small, concrete police post flying the Afghani flag just off the road. The soldiers straightened up and one of them moved out into the road. Larren braked, and too late he glimpsed the two large black cars hidden behind the police building.

Larren's first impulse was to stamp his foot down on the accelerator, but the rest of the soldiers were already moving forward. Their uniforms were a shabby, faded green, and some of their flat-topped caps were frayed around the peak, but their rifles were brand, spanking new and capably held. The man who was already in the road had the type of flat, mongoloid face that had been familiar in

Samarkand, and he had already seen the savage change in Larren's expression. He lifted his rifle sharply so that it aimed at Larren's head, and reluctantly Larren took his foot from the accelerator and pulled on the hand brake.

There were curt commands and Sharif got out of the car, protesting vigorously. While the Afghani argued the man with the mongoloid face made an unmistakable jerking movement with his rifle. His staring eyes had not once flickered away from Larren's face, and Larren had no choice but to obey the silent order and get out into the road. Caroline and Mannering received the same signs and slowly got out of the back of the car. Larren thought of the Smith & Wesson .38 that lay heavily in his jacket pocket, but against five levelled rifles a set of tiddly-winks would have been just as effective.

They were herded together around Sharif who was still arguing hotly. The young Afghani seemed to be possessed of a violently mounting fury, and abruptly he swung back to Larren.

"We are under arrest," he exploded. "They say that we fit the descriptions of four people wanted in connection with a murder commited in Kabul. The murder of Ray Gastoni. They are accusing us of Ray's murder!"

This was something that Larren had not expected, and he felt as though someone had just dealt him a sickening jab in the stomach. Now he understood the murderous look on Sharif's face, but before he could say anything to calm the younger man down the soldiers who surrounded them began hustling them all towards the police building. Sharif indulged in another fiery exchange of words and then said in English:

"There is a police officer from Kabul and another from Herat waiting to interrogate us."

Larren said nothing, for the two black cars hidden behind the building had already indicated that they could expect some higher authority from Herat. The senior men had obviously stayed out of sight in case their presence should arouse suspicion. By just leaving the normal amount of soldiers on the toll duty, they had lured the battered Moskvitch saloon into a trap, and despite his present feelings Larren had to admit that it had been casually but neatly done.

They were herded roughly into a small room in the police building, and here an even larger welcoming committee was waiting to receive them. There must have been nine or ten men in all, and the tiny room was grossly overcrowded. Behind a desk sat the Captain in charge of the post, and beside him a Sergeant. The rest of the occupants already in the room had obviously arrived in the two large cars from the north. There were two officers with high-rank tabs and the rest were underlings. One of the men, Larren guessed, was the authority from Herat, but it was the other who received his attention. He stared hard at the tall man masquerading as a police officer from Kabul, and although he had only seen that hard, cruel face once in the flesh he could not doubt its owner's identity. The horrified gasp that came from Mannering behind him was wholly unnecessary as an aid to recognition.

Korovin smiled, a gesture that seemed impossible for that cold, merciless face, and then said fondly in English:

"Good afternoon, Nevile. It is such a pleasure to have you back again. You know that I hate to lose an old friend, and you did not even stop to say good-bye."

He regarded Mannering for a moment, and then turned his smile upon Larren.

"And you, if I am not mistaken, are a British agent named Simon Larren. We have a large file detailing all your activities in our criminal archives in Moscow. I think that I can consider you as a very worthwhile bonus to my efforts."

16

The Fury of a Hawk

Larren wondered how the other man had learned his name, but he said nothing. Korovin watched him carefully and then repeated:

"Yes, Mister Larren, you make an excellent bonus. My department has nursed the ambition of receiving you into our loving care for a very long time. You have been personally responsible for many of our failings in the International field over recent years, and you have caused the deaths of some of our best men. It was you who killed Dressler in China. It was you who killed Stefan Kerensky on Barren Island in the Arctic. And it was you who killed Antonin Volkov in Istanbul. Yes, my friend, you have much to answer for, and we shall take care of you very well indeed."

Larren did not allow his expression to

change. He could have answered with similar details of Korovin's own career, remembered from the file in Whitehall, and with an equally impressive list of British agents listed as the Russian's kills. But he did not. He saw no reason to exchange compliments, or to boost the other man's ego. Instead he studied the cold face, noting the thin lips, the prominent cheek bones and the narrowed eyes, and he waited.

Korovin showed a flicker of annoyance, and then chose to ignore Larren and stare past him at Caroline and Sharif.

"And you — " The words stabbed at the young Afghani. "I think that you must be the man named Sardar Sharif, a sorry, misguided fool who works for the Americans, and more recently for the British. We knew that Larren had to have some local help, and as you were absent from Kabul when dearest Nevile was so brutally kidnapped from Samarkand we simply added up the facts."

Sharif looked like a human volcano on the verge of eruption, and one of the soldiers warningly moved a rifle into his range of vision. Korovin smiled and turned smoothly to Caroline.

"And you, young lady, I am afraid that I do not know your name. But no doubt we shall become better acquainted. It is a pity that you are so obviously another decadent capitalist spy, for you are almost pretty enough to be forgiven for any other crime."

Caroline said acidly: "What a shame that I cannot return your gallantry. You are ugly enough to be guilty of anything."

Korovin chuckled. "At least one of you has spirit. That is good. I deplore sullen and unresponsive faces. But perhaps I should have introduced myself first, before I expect an Englishman like Mister Larren to answer me. Perhaps you have already guessed, but my name is Vaslav Semyonovich Korovin. This gentleman beside me is Captain Mahmud, he is an officer from Police Headquarters in Herat, and has proved a very good friend of mine, or at least of my organization. It was only with his help that I was able to have you apprehended."

Larren turned his gaze on to the

Police Captain from Herat. Mahmud was a tall, strapping Afghani, very smart in his uniform and favouring a small dark moustache. He was the real authority here, and probably the only other man in the crowded room who would be able to speak English, for Korovin would not have been so outspoken if the rank and file had been able to follow his conversation. However, Mahmud returned Larren's stare blandly and chose to remain silent. He was not embarrassed by the fact that he had exposed himself as a man of dual loyalties working for the KGB.

Korovin went on: "And now we shall all return to Herat. There you will all be held in custody on suspicion of being involved in the murder of an American named Ray Gastoni. You, Mister Larren, fit the description of the man who was seen to leave the Pamir Hotel where the body was found. Also there is the question of a dead Afghani found this morning in the Kabul River which we think you may be able to explain. And finally there is the little matter of using a firearm in the street and causing a nasty accident to a car carrying three innocent Russian tourists." He paused there and glanced at Mahmud. "Larren is probably still carrying that firearm, and his dossier records that he also favours a knife. You had better search them all."

Mahmud nodded and translated the necessary orders. The four prisoners were swiftly searched and Larren was relieved of his automatic and the knife sheathed inside his sleeve. Korovin himself patted Caroline in all the likely places, acting with as much respect as a thorough search would allow, but the only other weapon was another knife found on Sharif.

When his turn came to be searched Mannering submitted meekly, and his white face looked towards Korovin. He wet his lips and then asked:

"How — how did you get to Herat to intercept us?"

"Very easily. This morning the fog had cleared in Kabul so I was able to get a domestic flight across country with Afghan Airways. I received a report from Khandahar to say that you had escaped

277

from the road block there and turned back. I assumed that you would find it too galling to return to Kabul, and that left you with no other choice but this road to Herat. I knew that in Herat I could rely on the very close co-operation of Captain Mahmud, and so I came ahead of you. On the plane I had plenty of time to think, and tried to place myself in your position. I decided that you would expect another attempt to be made at stopping your escape in Herat, and that your most likely move would be to leave the road before you reached the city — and so I came to meet you."

Larren had guessed as much. His moves had been predictable but even now he did not see what other choice he could have made. In the final stages of their flight they had only been able to hope for a lucky break, and the lucky break had failed to appear. Now there was only one question left and he asked sourly:

"How did you trace us to Khandahar?"

"I didn't," Korovin answered simply. "I should be interested to know how you managed to depart from Kabul in a Land Rover and then appear again in a black saloon, but you can tell me later how the switch was made. The main point that was in my favour was that there are so few road exits from Afghanistan. I could afford to cover them all. If you had tried to escape through the Khyber Pass you would have found another broken-down lorry in your path. Your escape was blocked whichever route you might have chosen to take."

Korovin smiled as he finished speaking, and then brushed his hands together in a sharp, business-like manner that indicated that all the preliminaries were over. He turned to Mahmud and said:

"And now we must leave for Herat. We will consider our next step when we have our prisoners safely locked up in the fortress."

Mahmud nodded and gave the orders. His voice was a crisp bark and it was clear that the men under him had a healthy respect for his temper. There was some confusion as they were herded out into the open again, but nothing from which Larren could take advantage. They were marched to the two large black cars and then separated, Mannering and Caroline being pushed towards the first car, and Larren and Sharif towards the one behind. Larren noted that there was also a third vehicle that he had not noticed before, an army Jeep that was parked close against the wall of the building. It was rapidly filled with armed soldiers and he guessed that they were to have an additional escort.

The two police cars were each large enough to hold six persons, although fully loaded they were a tight crush. Larren found himself on the back seat between Korovin and one of his aides, while Sharif was sandwiched between a second aide and the driver in front. In the leading car they could see Caroline in the back seat between Mahmud and one of his men, with Mannering presumably between the driver and another man in front. The convoy pulled out with the Jeep-load of soldiers bringing up the rear, and as they bumped out on to the road Larren glanced regretfully back at the battle-worn little Moskvitch saloon that was now being pushed out of the way by the men remaining on duty at the check-point.

The police car was smooth and powerful, eating up the miles, and Larren could not see a glimmer of hope in the present situation. He and Sharif had been considered the most dangerous pair and had been placed under Korovin's personal guard. The Russian was a killer who could not be fooled, and his two aides appeared equally as foreboding. They had both produced Russian Stetchkin automatics, and Larren guessed that they were the two KGB men who had flown with Korovin from Tashkent. They were silent, hostile men, and one of them had a large bruise over his eye which suggested that he might have been aboard the crashed car that Larren had shot up in Kabul. Their presence made the following escort of Afghani soldiers a completely irrelevant precaution.

In the front seat Sharif was still wrestling with his inner rage. His pride had been affronted at being addressed as a fool, and Korovin's devious twist of accusing them of Gastoni's murder had aggravated the canker of suppressed vengeance in his heart. His hooked face was again filled with hawk-like fury, and Larren was afraid that he might make some suicidal move. The silence allowed the Afghani's feelings to ferment, and so Larren chose to break it, hoping that he could distract the other man's mind.

He glanced at Korovin and said: "You knew my identity even before I was brought into that police post. I'd be interested to know how?"

"Mostly guesswork." Korovin could afford to be conversational. "We knew that Mannering had sent out a call for help. He managed to pass it through an attache at your British Embassy in Moscow. We had a reasonable suspicion that the call would be answered, and it seemed a good opportunity to eliminate another western agent. So we allowed Mannering to continue to Samarkand for treatment as planned. Then we learned from a source in London that you had departed for Afghanistan. The plot thickened, as the saying goes. You were much too good a prize to miss, and so I personally was sent to Samarkand to be on the spot when you arrived." He paused to make the wry gesture of a smile. "You moved much faster than I expected, Mister Larren, and did a very good job in getting Mannering out of the Soviet Union. I think we all made the mistake of under-estimating your abilities, a mistake that should not have happened in view of your past record. However, everything is ending satisfactorily. My position is still a little uncertain while I have to pose in this uniform, but Captain Mahmud is a genuine Afghani police officer, and with his help I think I can have you all taken back to the Soviet Union. After all we do have prior claims."

Larren nodded as though it was a matter of professional rather than personal interest, and then asked:

"And what about Nevile Mannering? What happens to him? I can't even make up my mind which side he's on?"

Korovin laughed. "Neither can we. In

283

fact I doubt now whether Nevile knows the answer to that question himself. He has changed sides so many times that he is of no use to anyone. I cannot really imagine why you took so much trouble to get him back. He may think he possesses valuable information, but I assure you that he is suffering from self-delusion. But, of course, you were not to know the man that he had become until it was too late."

That, Larren thought bitterly, is the bloody understatement of the year. He momentarily forgot his purpose in making conversation and stared gloomily out of the window.

The drive continued in silence, and the next interuption came abruptly from the man at the wheel. He slowed the car and all heads looked round. Behind them the escorting Jeep had stopped and the Afghani soldiers were climbing out on to the road. Korovin scowled, spat out a Russian oath and then an order. Their driver backed the car up towards the Jeep until they could all see what had happened. The escort vehicle had developed a flat tyre on the offside wheel. One of the soldiers came away from the Jeep and approached the car with an apologetic expression on his face, and Korovin treated him to a string of scathing words. Then he gave another order to their driver.

The police car moved off again and left the stranded Jeep behind. The leading police car with Caroline and Mannering had not noticed anything amiss and was now far ahead. The convoy had broken up, but Korovin sensed Larren's thoughts and made a warning movement of his head.

"Be wise, Mister Larren, the Jeep was not really necessary, and the fact that the fools have broken down does not change anything. My two comrades are professional men."

Larren looked at the bruised face of the silent KGB man beside him and conceded that Korovin was right. Their driver put his foot down and set out to overhaul the car in front, but no one seemed unduly worried. There was no need.

As they neared Herat there was a surprise change in the landscape. The road became a straight avenue between single lines of tall, full-grown pine trees. The brown plains continued on either side for a few more miles and then fell behind. The road passed through a large, park-like area of more pines and Larren realized that they were entering Herat. The third city of Afghanistan lay on the far side of the park. The leading police car was still out of sight ahead of them, and the dusty pines appeared to be deserted.

Sharif moved. Larren had feared some hot-headed action from the smouldering Afghani, but even he was taken by surprise. It was a fanatical, hopeless effort, and Larren was never to know what desperate line of reasoning lay behind its inspiration. Perhaps Sharif genuinely believed that they had a fighting chance now that their car was isolated from the convoy. Or perhaps the primitive code of blood for blood had caused him to try and kill them all in order to satisfy his honour. There had been something of idolatry in his relationship with Ray Gastoni, and he may have considered those last, swiftly-passing miles as the only opportunity that he would now get for exacting his revenge. But whatever the thought in his mind he chose to act rather than to tamely submit to any further indignities that Korovin had in store.

He struck with the lightning savagery of a falling hawk. The KGB man on his right was totally unprepared for the elbow that suddenly smashed up into his face, his head was knocked back and he uttered a harsh, choking cry through his bleeding teeth. In the same moment Sharif's left arm was flung out like a lashing battering ram to knock the driver sideways. Twisting and lunging, the young Afghani grabbed at the wheel, hauling it round and sending the car careering straight at the pine trees. The KGB man at Larren's side yelled hoarsely and jerked up the big Stetchkin automatic in his hand to splatter the Afghani's brains, and then Larren had to take a desperate, supporting hand. He grappled with the KGB man to force the gun away, but was hampered by Korovin who reacted just as swiftly and seized him from behind. Larren could not defend himself and still hang on to that lethal gun hand, and so he was helpless as Korovin thrust both hands under his arms and then locked them behind his neck in a tight full nelson. In the squashed confines of the car there was no room to throw the man off. Then the KGB man in the front seat rallied himself and fired three bullets at point-blank range along the ridge of Sharif's spine.

The Afghani must have been killed instantly, but the damage was done. The car had been travelling fast and hit the edge of the road with a force that literally hurled it into the air. The three shots slammed Sharif's hideously arched body even tighter against the wheel and no one could control the car. The pines loomed up and the KGB man who had fired the fatal shots screamed and tried to duck his face beneath his arm. Larren glimpsed the yawning trunks like a vast mouth of straight, gapped teeth, and he too ducked as the jaws closed in an almighty crash.

The next few seconds were indescribable in any detail. Larren felt as though he had been struck on all sides and thrown in all directions at once. There was a sensation of spinning and tumbling in a violently explosive nightmare that was made up of falling trees, breaking glass and heavy bodies crushing on top of him. The whole world revolved and crashed for what might have been the second or third time, and then there was blackness.

★ ★ ★

The car had completely felled two of the pines, snapping them off as though they had been saplings. The bonnet was crushed in like a pug's nose, hissing and steaming in its broken agony. Every window and piece of glass had been completely shattered, and the bodywork was dented and crumpled where it had rolled across the hard earth, bouncing off more of the pine trunks before it had come to its final stop. It lay completely upside down like a helpless beetle, while

17

Herat

The dust gradually subsided, and settled back to the brown earth like a gently falling screen. The whirling wheels spun more slowly, losing momentum, and at last becoming still. The hissing and gurgling sounds from the ruptured radiator faded and died as the last of the escaping water drained away and there was a deep, oppressive hush. Five minutes passed. Five empty, paralysed minutes of uncertain time, and then there was a faint movement from inside the overturned car.

Simon Larren opened his eyes. He was crushed between two heavy bodies, he was half-suffocated, his head ached and his brain was too dizzy to grasp more than the immediate pains. His leg felt as though it was broken and his ribs as though they had caved in.

There were two sharply defined points of pain cutting into his cheek, and as the haze cleared from his mind he realized that his face was pressed hard against Korovin's chest, and that the twin points of pain were the bright buttons from the borrowed uniform grinding into his flesh. Korovin was also alive, for he could feel the breathing movement of the man's chest.

There was the smell of blood, and death — and petrol.

Larren tried to move, coughed, and then fell back. He twisted his face so that he could breathe more easily and rallied his strength for another try. Then there was a groaning sound and the weight above him shifted. The job was easier now and he managed to struggle out from between Korovin and the KGB aide who had been above him, crawling over Korovin's unconscious body. He twisted so that he could sit upright and looked to the groaning KGB man.

Dark eyes stared back at him from the bruised face. There was a fresh cut above that bruise that gave birth to trickles of red over the blue and yellow flesh, and the man's left arm was twisted at a broken angle. He stopped groaning and shakily raised his right hand so that Larren could see it. The hand still retained the big Stetchkin automatic. The gun might have weighed a ton, and the KGB man had to concentrate hard as he tried to point it at Larren's heart. Larren's counter-move was equally slow and shaky, and the whole dazed and uncertain tableau was acted out as though underwater or in a slow-motion film. There was a stab of fire across Larren's chest as he lifted his arm, but once he had raised it the chopping blow fell more easily. The KGB man had the Stetchkin levelled, but he didn't have the strength to pull the trigger. The hard edge of Larren's palm took the side of his neck, and the eyes that were partly glazed became fully glassy. It was a weak chop, but against the injured man it was enough, and as the KGB man slumped back into a heap Larren feebly wrested the automatic from his fingers.

Larren was in control now, and unsteadily he surveyed the wreckage.

The car was upside down, and the front both smelled and looked like a butcher's slaughter-house that had been struck by a bomb. Sharif had been dead before the crash, but the police driver and the KGB man who had shot him in the back had not survived him by many seconds. Those in the front of the car had taken the full force of the crash. The engine had been partially pushed through from the bonnet to crush and trap the legs of the two men who had been seated, and now they dangled head downwards from the mangled wreckage like hooked carcasses. The slack lolling of the heads showed that both necks had been snapped as they were thrown forward by the initial impact. Sharif's body had fallen on to the inside roof of the car, which was now the floor, and his chest had been smashed and all but impaled by the steering wheel which had punched him aside. Strangely there was no pain on the Afghani's face, just dark savagery, the hawk-like eyes still gleaming with dead defiance.

There was still the ominous smell of petrol.

The rear door had burst open and had almost been torn away. Larren crawled through the gap across Korovin's unconscious form and continued to make painful progress on his hands and knees for several yards. Then he found a pine tree and hauled himself up. The effort caused a dozen stabs of agony, but despite his fears there was nothing broken. His left leg sagged under his weight but did not collapse.

His strength began to return and his mind cleared towards normal. He looked at the wrecked car, and at the snapped, sap-oozing trunks of the felled pine trees and knew that he had been very lucky indeed. By being in the centre of the back seat he had occupied the best position of all in the car, cushioned and protected on either side by the bodies of Korovin and his aide. He wondered whether Sharif had realized that he would be the one most likely to survive, and whether the Afghani had deliberately died in the hope of giving him this one slim chance, but it was a question that would never be answered. Larren stared at the wreckage for a moment longer, remembering that Sharif was a Moslem, and then said softly:

"Allah, be kind to him."

And then he turned and limped unsteadily away through the dusty forest of pine trees.

★ ★ ★

He was still too shaken for any positive, constructive thought, but one fact stood out sharply in his mind. It was imperative that he wasted no time in leaving the scene of the crash. At any moment Captain Mahmud in the leading police car might suspect that something was amiss and return, or alternatively the escorting Jeep full of Afghani soldiers might reappear from the south. Either way Larren had to be well clear.

His leg ached abominably as he stumbled through the trees, and he guessed that whenever he was able to stop and examine his left knee he would find that it was nothing but one great bruise. His chest also hurt with every breath, which indicated several cracked or bruised ribs, and he vaguely remembered that he had been hurled hard against the back of the seat in front of him when the car had left the road. The car was soon out of sight behind him, hidden by the curtain of pine trunks, and he was tempted to stop. Every bone and muscle in his body was begging him to lie down and rest, but his mind was in control and his mind insisted that he go on.

The pine-tree park covered a wide area, but at last Larren emerged into the dirt streets of Herat. As yet there were no sounds of pursuit and the shadows were gathering into dusk. High mud walls replaced the enclosing pines, but the street was almost deserted. The few people that he encountered stared curiously but hurried past. A woman veiled like a ghost in an enveloping black tent that began like a close skull cap and then flared out into a long, pleated robe that trailed to the ground saw him approach and turned fearfully up a side alley. She might have been sixteen or sixty, and even her eyes were hidden behind a narrow lace mesh. A man in a large white turban and wrapped in a long and coarse grey blanket watched with suspicious eyes, but made no move to question or hinder as Larren lurched along. It was obvious that he was in one of the poorer quarters of the city where a lone, wandering white man was a complete stranger, and Larren felt as prominent as a sore thumb.

He kept walking, despite his protesting leg, and slowly tried to calculate his chances. On the face of it they were almost nil. He was free, but Caroline Brand and Nevile Mannering were still prisoners, and Sharif who had so often been the cause of their salvation was dead. Larren had only his own resources but he was badly battered, and without Sharif he was almost helpless. He did not even speak the local language. The whole operation had turned into a complete and utter mess, and there was nothing that could be salvaged except perhaps his own escape, and even that was doubtful.

Thinking was a slow process, but it kept his mind away from his aches and hurts and so he forced himself to continue. His chances of remaining free were slim, and he guessed that they must depend entirely upon how openly Captain Mahmud would dare to aid Korovin. The Afghani officer knew that the Russian was an imposter wearing a faked or stolen uniform, and so there had to be a limit to the extent of his co-operation. It was a small matter to show his face at the checkpoint and use his weight to make a phoney arrest, but it might be beyond his powers to order a full-scale search of Herat in order to bring about Larren's recapture. And even if he did possess that authority Mahmud might be reluctant to use it. For eventually he would have to explain his actions to his superiors. Already the crashed police car would have complicated matters and the Herat police officer might well be having second thoughts on the wisdom of taking more orders from the KGB. A lot would depend upon what control Korovin could exercise over Mahmud, but on this question Larren could only speculate. He could only hope that Korovin's control was minimal, and that Mahmud's first and most pressing consideration would be his own continued position as an officer of the Afghani police.

Whatever the odds one thing was plain, in his western clothes Larren was too conspicuous, and if he wanted to remain free he would at least have to do something about his appearance to merge more naturally with the general background. He was entering the centre of the city now and was attracting more stares, although most of the Afghanis were too dignified to stare for any length of time. The first shock of despair had worn off, and although he had no real hope Larren was not the kind of man to give in before the end. He turned up a narrow alley between close mud walls, and after some moments found a recessed doorway where he could wait unseen.

An old woman shuffled past, another shadowy ghost in her flowing robe, but she saw nothing. Five minutes passed and then two small boys came up the alleyway, gossiping together. Larren stopped breathing and fought to bear the pain in his chest as they wandered by his hiding place. Small boys were notoriously inquisitive and alert, but these two were mercifully arguing and noticed nothing. Another wait, and then a man approached, a tall, regal old man moving slowly but purposefully.

Larren tensed. He knew that he would not be proud of himself afterwards, but he was glad that the man was old and slow. In his present state a younger man might have been too much. No one else entered the alley, and as the old man drew level Larren stepped from his place of concealment and struck once with the hard edge of his hand. The old man tumbled silently and Larren caught him beneath the arms and lowered him against the wall. He quickly helped himself to the old man's turban and the long blanket-like robe that was easily unravelled. And then in a spasm of conscience he pulled a wad of Afghani notes from his pocket and tucked a generous payment into the old man's shirt front. Then he left the alley and hurried on his way.

He kept his head bowed, for his face was whiter and lacked the sharp hooked nose of the true Afghani. The dark stain that he had used previously had long since worn off after his second crossing of the Oxus, but he felt that in the darkness the turban and the blanket robe would be sufficient for him to pass unnoticed. His next move was still undecided, and again he could think of nothing except to keep moving. Otherwise his left leg might become stiff and refuse to let him move at all.

Unexpectedly he came out on to a wide main street that was dimly lighted and moderately busy. The dark, cave-like shops on either side appeared to be full of nothing but great piles of second-hand clothing, and many of the bundles had over-flowed on to the dirt pavement where small groups of veiled women knelt and pulled them apart. A pony trotted by pulling a brightly painted trap that carried another mysteriously veiled female passenger behind the Afghani driver, and a youth rode by on an ancient bicycle. The only motorized traffic to be seen was a large lorry standing at the far end of the street, brightly painted in blue, yellow and green. There were plenty of pedestrians, but none of them spared Larren a second glance. To his left an attractive blue and gold tiled mosque with four tall minarets blocked off the end of the street, and to his right above the intervening row of shops he could see the lofty, brick-red towers of a massive old-fashioned fort.

For a moment he looked longingly towards the mosque. He badly needed to rest and sleep, and the mosque was a tempting sanctuary. It was usual to find old men sleeping in the shaded courtyards, and it was possible that he could relax unnoticed. It was also possible that he would make some obvious mistake such as failing to wash his feet and be denounced as an imposter which could prove fatal. He turned the other way and limped slowly towards the fort.

As his first view had suggested it was a massive place, a crumbling citadel built upon a red brown hill rising in the centre of the city. The walls, and several of its huge, circular towers, were broken down, but even in disrepair it was still an impressive and formidable sight. Larren knew nothing of its history, but guessed that it must have witnessed the rampaging of Ghengis Khan. In the thirteenth century there was no city in Afghanistan that had not been over-run by the Mongol hordes.

For a moment he stared up at the big squared structure, and then abruptly he heard the sound of a car engine and the impatient honking of a car's horn. He turned and saw a large black saloon speeding towards him, and abruptly in the same moment he remembered Korovin's words to Mahmud back at the checkpoint. Korovin had suggested that the prisoners be taken to Herat and locked in the fortress. There could only be one fortress in Herat, and as the memories tumbled into place Larren decided that he did not need a closer look to identify the black car.

However, there was no escape without making himself obvious by running, and

Larren was hardly capable of running anyway. He hesitated for a fraction of a second and then chose to rely on his disguise. He limped clear of the police car as it came up behind him and pressed close to a group of men who had been haggling around a nearby stall laden down with red pomegranates. The men paused in their conversation to watch the arrival of the police car with polite interest, and making sure that his face was in shadow Larren watched with them.

The car stopped and Mahmud got out, a grim-faced but impressive figure in his uniform. From behind there came the sound of another engine and then the escorting Jeep appeared. Mahmud walked towards it snapping orders and the Afghani soldiers tumbled out of the back with their rifles raised, making a fine show of speed and efficiency to compensate for their earlier mistakes. The activity became confused, but then Caroline Brand was forced to get out of the front of the police car. From the back emerged Mannering, followed by Korovin and the KGB man whom Larren had been obliged to knock unconscious only shortly before. Korovin looked pale and unsteady and there was blood in his hair from a cut above his right ear. He had lost his cap and his borrowed uniform was streaked and stained. The aide with the broken arm was still only semi-conscious and needed support from one of the soldiers to hold him upright. When they were all clear of the car Mahmud barked another string of commands and both the police car and the Jeep reversed into twin three-point turnings and sped back the way they had come. The whole party then began to move towards the fortress with Caroline and Mannering being propelled at rifle point. Mannering was cowed and beaten, but Caroline walked straight with her head thrown contemptuously back.

Larren had already worked out the obvious reasons for Mahmud's long delay in arriving at Herat. The Police Captain had become aware that something was wrong and had turned back to find the second police car crashed in the pine trees. Probably he had been obliged to wait until the following Jeep arrived before he had sufficient men to right the car and disentangle the bodies. Or, more probably, he had waited for the Jeep in order to organize an immediate search of the pine woods for the one missing prisoner. Whatever the exact reasons he had clearly spent time at the scene of the crash, and now he had despatched the car and the Jeep back again to recover the bodies and pick up any of his men who had been forced to remain behind to make space for Korovin and his injured aide. The real questions only concerned the future, and depended on the character and quality of the Afghani Police Captain. On his next moves would hang Larren's fate, but Larren did not know enough about the man to predict what those next moves would be.

There was one comforting ray of thought, and that was that even if Mahmud did launch a full-scale search he would hardly expect the man he hunted to be lurking in the close vicinity of the fortress that was to have been his prison. By chance Larren's steps had led him to what was probably the safest area in which to take a rest, if only he could find somewhere to sit down.

And then another thought flickered in his brain as he watched the last of the Afghani soldiers disappearing into the fortress. He was on the spot, and now, when his enemies would expect him to be somewhere in hiding and licking his wounds, was the best opportunity he would ever have to affect a rescue. Despite its size the fortress was crumbling in too many places to be invulnerable, and he still had the Stetchkin automatic he had taken from the KGB man in his pocket.

He could only think of one move at a time now, and he deliberately chose to ignore the question of how he would proceed afterwards, even if he was successful in getting Caroline and Mannering out of the fortress. Instead he drew his shrouding blanket closer around him and began to circle round towards the back of those giant walls. His physical hurts were something that would have to be ignored until later, and he concentrated all his mind on the problem of forcing an entry.

18

The Fortress

From the back the fort gave the impression of an unused ruin, there were no guards and the round, buttressing towers were a silent silhouette against the dark night sky. There were eight of the towers, one guarding each corner, and one placed along the centre of each of the four walls. To his right much of the walls had crumbled, but to his left they were solid and in a better state of repair. Larren stared thoughtfully for a moment, and then chose to make his climb close by the corner tower to his left, as it looked as though only that part of the fort could still be fit for use.

The path that encircled the back of the fort showed no other signs of life, and he could see no indications that he was being observed from the mud and brick houses that formed the tumbledown area behind him. Even so he hesitated, but then again he forced all thoughts of failure from his mind. His doubts about Mannering's value to the West, although increased since his conversation with Korovin, were no longer important. There was still Caroline Brand to consider, and Larren knew that for her sake alone he would have to make a rescue attempt. And in any case, his chances of affecting a rescue at this stage were perhaps as good as his chances of escaping alone. The future was bleak and held no room for logic and cold reason, impulse and instinct were taking their place. The Whitehall-dominated area of his mind was dulled, but the remaining factors were compelling him to go after Caroline. It was not that he was in love with her, at least not permanently, but there were strong emotional links from both present and past that could not be broken, and he knew that she was worth a dozen Nevile Mannerings. He stared up at the massive walls that framed her prison, and abruptly he realized that the code name for the original mission was still appropriate. Speed and surprise were his only possible allies now, and to succeed he had to strike fast.

Without any further hesitation he moved towards the fort. He had to descend into a dry shallow moat, and wrinkled his nose as he realized that he was passing through another outdoor Afghani lavatory. He climbed up the steep slope to the foot of the tower, wincing and gritting his teeth as he banged his injured knee, and then he huddled for a moment in the patch of shadow where the tower joined the wall. He looked back and saw two men coming along the path that he had just left, but they walked by without noticing that anything was taking place. Larren watched them depart and then carefully freed himself from the blanket-like robe that concealed his ordinary clothes. He almost fell back into the foul-smelling ditch that was the empty moat, but regained his balance just in time. He left the robe at the foot of the tower, checked over the heavy Stetchkin automatic and returned it to his pocket, and then faced the wall that loomed above him.

At close quarters it was a much more formidable barrier, but there were enough gaps in the ancient brickwork to make it an easy climb for a fit man with any kind of commando training, Larren had the training but he was no longer a fit man. Again he tried to will the pain from his chest and from his knee away from his mind, concentrating solely on the wall. He climbed it slowly, like a weakening fly, and had to rely mostly on the strength of his arms and fingers. He dared not trust his full weight to his left leg, and apart from steadying his balance the whole limb was a useless agony. His chest was another sea of pain as he pulled himself up by his arms, but at least there was the comforting thought that his ribs could only be bruised. If they had been cracked the climb would have been impossible.

The fortress had stood for centuries, and the deteriorations of siege and time had left an ample number of holds in the brickwork, and gradually Larren neared the top of the wall. When his searching fingers gripped over the edge he was almost spent and feared that he was too late. Pain and exhaustion filled his whole body, but the only choice now was between falling and going on. He uttered a fervent prayer of gratitude as he found a hold for his right foot, a good deep hold that enabled him to give a hard thrust and then drag himself on to the top of the wall.

He was still in the shadow cast by the corner tower, and so he continued to sprawl face down, pressed flat and panting hard for breath. He was sweating and the brick dust that lay along the top of the wall stuck uncomfortably to the palms of his hands and his cheek. There had been no outcry of alarm and so he lay for a full five minutes to recover his strength before he twisted his face around to look inside the fort.

There were some modern additions in the shape of barrack blocks and offices built along the inside of the old walls, and there was a new concrete building standing more centrally and flying the Afghani flag. Electric lights were supported on tall poles to give some shadowy relief to the open spaces between the buildings, and the central building was also brightly lit. There was a soldier with a bayonet fixed to his rifle standing on sentry duty outside the central building, and on the opposite side of the fort Larren could see a similar silhouette standing in the open gateway. The rest of the fortress appeared to be deserted.

Larren had to force himself to think now. Very little time had elapsed since he had watched Caroline and Mannering being ushered into the fort, and the odds were that the whole party, including Korovin and Mahmud, would be in the lighted central building. There would be questions, paperwork and delay before the prisoners could be placed in the cells, and possibly some initial interrogation by Korovin. Larren was in no immediate danger of discovery, and so he chose to wait.

Another five minutes passed before he was rewarded. Then the doors of

the central building opened and the
sentry moved smartly to one side with
a salute. Through the open doorway
came Caroline Brand, still looking pertly
defiant. Behind her was Mannering with
slumped shoulders and a dejected face,
and then Mahmud and two armed
soldiers. The whole party came directly
towards Larren, then turned left to walk
past almost immediately below the spot
where he lay watching. They came to
a stop outside one of the barrack-like
blocks midway along the wall, below the
centre tower to Larren's right, and after
a short delay while the door was unlocked
the group moved inside. Voices emerged,
but not clearly enough for Larren to
distinguish what was being said, and then
Mahmud reappeared alone and walked
back to the central office. The Police
Captain's face was blank and revealed
nothing as he passed briefly under one
of the lights, but he was moving briskly.
When the doors of the central building
had closed behind him silence reigned
once more, and the fort resumed its
deserted appearance except for the two

motionless sentries.

Larren's left leg was becoming stiff and he knew that he could afford to waste no more time. He had already gained an extra card by observing the exact location of the cells where Caroline and Mannering were being held, and now he had to make his gamble. He licked his lips and spat out some of the clinging dust, and then began to wriggle cautiously along the top of the wall. He stayed flat as he left the shadow of the corner tower and kept as close as possible to the outer edge of the wall with the sheer drop into the dry moat immediately to his right. Gradually he inched closer to the ruined centre tower, and when he reached it he had no difficulty in dropping down on to the flat roof of the cell block below. He crouched there with his back pressed against the ancient wall, and decided that from now on the heavy Stetchkin automatic would be more reassuring in his hand than in his pocket.

The squared hulk of the central building was now screening him from the view of the two sentries, but he had to remember that Mahmud had left two more of his men somewhere below to guard the two prisoners. With that thought in mind he moved silently and almost on tiptoe across the cell block roof. He crouched low for a brief reconnaissance over the edge and assured himself that the ground below was empty of life. The cell block door was closed, but there was a light from the small window and the two armed guards were obviously inside.

Larren drew a deep breath, and then winced through his teeth as his chest expanded. However, after the agony of climbing the outer wall his activities now were comparative child's play, and without any further hesitation he lowered himself over the edge of the roof and dropped to the ground. All he had was the gun and a prayer, and he was dependent upon speed and luck.

He stood with his back against the wall for a second and looked quickly through the small square window. The two Afghani soldiers were sitting at a bare table with their rifles leaning close at hand. One man was steadily eating at a large sandwich of unleavened bread with some greasy-looking filling, while the other gazed thoughtfully at one of the two closed doors behind them. Each door had a bolt and a padlock, and a small barred window at face height, and Larren did not need two guesses to know who lay behind them. He tightened his lips, opened the door and went in.

The two soldiers turned calmly, and then went rigid. Then the man with his mouth full of bread made a grab for his rifle as Larren closed the door. Larren took a swift pace forward and thrust the automatic close into the startled face. The soldier choked over the bread in his mouth and then reluctantly drew back. No words had been spoken, but words were unnecessary. The automatic, the hard face, and the savage blaze in the grey-green eyes all carried their own warning.

Carefully Larren picked up the nearest rifle and moved it clear. He circled the table and removed the second rifle, and the two soldiers watched dumbly with uncertain eyes. The only sound came from the man who had been interrupted while eating as he faintly coughed and spluttered. Larren stepped back so that he could watch them both and then indicated that they should rise. Slowly, like weak old men, they obeyed. Larren made another silent, circling motion with his hand, and they turned around. Deftly Larren pushed the Stetchkin on to safety with his thumb, and then used his gun-laden fist like a club to deal the first man a savage blow behind the left ear. The soldier went sprawling over the table and his companion turned in alarm. His mouth came sharply open, but Larren's fingers jabbed swiftly into the exposed stomach to force out the breath that would have been needed for a shout. The man gasped instead as he doubled over, and then Larren clubbed him hard over the back of the neck.

Larren stepped back to let the second guard slide in an unconscious heap to the floor, and for a moment he froze and listened, facing the outer door with the automatic still levelled. A certain amount of noise had been unavoidable, but after a short pause he was satisfied that nothing had been heard. He checked that both soldiers were out cold, and then turned to face the cells. He was weak and unsteady, but his lips framed a faint smile.

Caroline was watching him through the small square of bars, her eyes were anxious and it was a moment before she could speak. Then she said softly:

"Simon, I almost expected you to do something like this. You seem to make a habit of saving me from uncomfortable prisons."

Larren's mind groped, and then the memory came back. There had been similar circumstances long ago in the Caribbean. He dredged up another smile and answered:

"I think that derives from your awkward habit of getting into uncomfortable prisons."

He searched for the keys and Caroline pointed out the large ring hanging from a nail by the door. After that it took only a moment to unfasten the big padlock and shoot back the bolt on the cell door. Caroline came out, and only then did Larren realize that Mannering had been locked in the same cell. The ex-diplomat's pasty face appeared behind Caroline's shoulder, hesitated and then hung back in the cell doorway. Caroline moved swiftly over to the window to keep watch, but Mannering made no further move. Larren said impatiently:

"Hurry it up. We haven't got time to hang about."

Mannering stared at him, and then blurted through white lips:

"Larren, this time I know that you must be mad. It is suicide for you to come here, and even if we can escape — where can we go? We have tried running in every direction and we have failed. Everything is finished. This is insanity. We saw the body of your Afghani friend dragged out of that crashed car. Sharif is dead, Larren. Without him we have no chance at all!"

Larren said curtly: "I know about Sharif, but we'll just have to do without him. I came here for Caroline, but the three of us stand as much chance of escaping as two, and at this stage I'm damned if I'll leave you behind after all that we've been through on your behalf."

"But I don't want to come. Korovin will only catch up with us again. It's all so pointless and we're only making things worse for ourselves. In any case, where can we go?"

"North." It was an impulse answer and as good as any. "We'll take the north road up towards the Soviet frontier. Korovin may not expect that. Before we get there we can turn west to Persia. We'll steal a car or horses if we can, and if not we'll try it on foot. Either way you're coming along."

"No! Not this time. Go where you please, but I've had enough."

Larren grabbed the shorter man by the front of his jacket and dragged him bodily out of the cell. He rammed the nose of the automatic hard into Mannering's stomach and said viciously:

"If you insist on staying behind then I'll assume that you've been a bloody Communist all along, and that'll be enough excuse to blow a hole right through you. At this range your own stomach will muffle the shot."

Mannering gaped at him and his face was sick. Larren shook him hard and then half threw him across the room to the door. Caroline caught and steadied him, and then said quietly:

"Go easy, Simon. Nevile will come if you give him time to adjust. Remember that he's suffering from a nervous breakdown."

She gave Mannering a smile, and then nodded to Larren to lead the way. Her blue eyes held an expression that was partly a warning and partly an assurance that she could handle their reluctant fellow-traveller. Larren hesitated, but getting rough with Mannering had hurt his own chest so badly that he could only nod his own head in return and then move past her to the door. The open space outside was clear and he said briefly:

"Our luck's holding. Let's go."

He opened the cell door and all three of them squeezed out into the night.

324

Mannering came last and with no more argument as Caroline tugged gently at his sleeve. He made a pathetic attempt to save face by pretending a response to Caroline's smile, but they all knew that his resistance had capitulated under Larren's threats. Larren let them pass and then closed the door behind them, shutting in the light as they flattened against the wall. He pointed upwards and they understood.

Caroline had already realized that Larren was in pain, and it was she who scrambled first on to the cell-block roof. Larren was about to urge Mannering up next, but unexpectedly Mannering cupped his hands to offer a foothold. Larren hesitated and then accepted the offer. Caroline helped him from above and he crawled back on to the roof with an effort, gasping from the pain in his chest. He stayed on his hands and knees and heard Caroline hissing urgently to Mannering, and for a moment he thought that the other man had tricked him and ran back into the cell block. Anger surged through him and he determined to go back, but then Caroline checked him and he realized that Mannering was still below. He came up with Caroline's help, puffing clumsily, and then all three of them moved back to the outer wall.

Larren had all but relinquished leadership now, for Caroline was the strongest of the three. She bit her lip as she saw the drop that awaited them outside the fort, and then demanded the stolen turban that Larren was still wearing. He handed it over and she quickly shook out the long fold of tightly bound cloth into a makeshift rope.

They climbed on to the top of the wall, and Larren lowered himself down the far side. He did not enjoy making the first descent, for he still feared some kind of betrayal from Mannering, but he knew that he was not capable of another full-distance climb and so he had no choice. It needed both Caroline and Mannering to hold his weight. There were over three yards of material in the unravelled turban, and by the time he was dangling from the lower end his feet were only a short drop from the foot of the wall. His outstretched arms made the strain on his chest an agony of hot fire, and he was almost incapable of transferring his body to the face of the wall to climb the remainder of the way down. He slithered down the harsh brickwork and only just succeeded in staying upright at the bottom. There he leaned against the wall, feeling weak and dizzy, and waited for Mannering to join him.

Caroline came last. She took off her coat and shoes and dropped them into Mannering's hands, and as there was no suitable anchor point for the turban rope she climbed down the full length of the wall, clinging to the cracks in the brickwork with her fingers and stockinged toes. She managed slowly but easily, and smiled in the darkness when she was able to re-don her coat and shoes. They descended the steep slope at the foot of the wall and her smile only faded when they had to pick their way through the droppings of human excrement that littered the dry bed of the moat. They climbed up on to the path, and in the darkness no one saw their escape as they hurried away from the massive shadow of the fortress to lose themselves in the streets of Herat.

19

The Ruined Tower

The pursuit caught them within half an hour.

Larren had hoped for time and luck but both were denied them, and as they left Herat they failed to find any kind of motorized vehicle that they might have comandeered to aid their escape. There was not even a donkey and trap left unattended. The dirt streets between the low mud or stone walls of the buildings were dark and silent, and at that hour of the night practically deserted. Herat was ancient, with a long and varied history, already old when it had witnessed the marching legions of Alexander the Great on their conquest of Asia, but now it was almost a ghost city, lamenting for its lost but not forgotten past.

The stars were bright and the air was cold as the three fugitives hurried along.

The maze of empty, mysterious streets forced them to take many twists and turnings, but they headed as much as possible in a northerly direction which they hoped would lead them on to the main road north that would take them back towards Mazar-i-Sharif and the Soviet frontier. They succeeded only in getting themselves lost, and then ahead of them rose more traces of the past. They saw six giant towers with broken tops thrusting up into the star-filled sky. They were the minarets of some long destroyed mosque, and colossal reminders that despite its present appearance Herat had once enjoyed its golden age as the third largest city of Afghanistan. Two of the towers were a little to their left, but they were on a long straight road that was taking them directly towards the four main towers immediately ahead, and it was then that they heard the sound of car engines snarling through the night and coming up fast from behind.

Larren halted and twisted round to see the first set of headlights swinging into the far end of the road. There was a convoy of at least three vehicles and their presence and purpose needed no explanation. Larren swore savagely with no respect for Caroline's ears, and automatically cocked the heavy Stetchkin in his hand. Mannering made a panic move and grabbed quickly at his arm.

"No, Larren. Don't be a fool!"

Larren would have hurled him aside, but Caroline was still thinking clearly. They had been hurrying past a long wall on their left that separated them from some kind of park or pine-shaded gardens, and then she saw that there was an opening in the wall a few yards ahead. She snapped quickly:

"Simon, this way!"

Larren hesitated, but then Mannering let go of his arm and began to run frantically after Caroline who was already retreating to the gateway. The blazing headlights were coming up fast, blinding him, and Larren turned to stumble after Mannering. He cursed his limp and the painful throbbing in his knee, and all three of them tumbled through the gap in the wall only seconds before the convoy sped past. Then another disaster fouled all their hopes. Larren tripped and fell full length over a sleeping watchman huddled under a blanket just inside the gateway and the man woke with a yowl of alarm.

Larren landed hard on his chest and was crippled by the murderous crash of agony from his already bruised ribs. He lay momentarily helpless, his mouth open and gasping for breath and a flood of hot tears burning in his eyes. He was incapable of stopping the terrified man from running out of the gateway and into the road. Mannering was too slow and Caroline was too far away.

He heard the squealing of brakes sounding above the startled man's cries as the convoy of passing cars slithered to a halt, and weakly tried to crawl to his knees. He had dropped the heavy Stetchkin automatic and he saw Caroline stoop to pick it up. She went back to the gateway, briefly glanced through, and then came back to help Larren to his feet.

"It's Mahmud's police car," she said

briefly. "And about a dozen Afghani soldiers in three Jeeps."

Larren was on his feet, but he was still too winded to answer. From the roadway came the sound of car doors being opened and slammed and a noisy exchange of shouts and orders. The frightened Afghani who had been flushed by Larren's clumsy plunge through the gateway was obviously being called upon to halt, and Larren knew that it could be only a matter of moments before Mahmud had learned the facts. There was a rush of booted feet that made them think that all was already lost, and they crouched low behind the wall as two soldiers ran past the gateway with fixed bayonets on their rifles. They heard the struggle as the unfortunate watch-man was apprehended, but they did not wait to see him brought back. Larren was capable of movement and they continued their flight.

They had entered a large expanse of dusty gardens, densely shaded by pine trees and with well-tended paths and carefully led irrigation channels threading

in all directions. Caroline was helping
Larren now as they hurried along, and
it galled Larren to realize that he was
now the biggest handicap to their
escape. Mannering kept close beside
them, panting and stumbling frequently
as he looked over his shoulder. They
could hear shouts and the sounds of
pursuit as the soldiers entered the garden
in the darkness behind them, and above
it all the crisp voice of Mahmud leading
the hunt.

They reached an intersection of paths,
a starlit space clear of the black gloom
beneath the pines, and for a second they
were halted by indecision. To their right
rose one of the huge ruined towers that
they had seen from the road, a massive
construction of crumbling brick over a
hundred feet high. To their left they
could also see the dome of a partly ruined
mosque looming above the pines.

That second's pause was almost fatal.
The searching soldiers had spread
themselves out but were thrusting quickly
through the pines. The net was closing
and the three fugitives left the path in

almost the same instant that the first of the soldiers emerged from the gloom. The hunt had caught up with them and Larren dragged his two companions down into a shallow but dry irrigation ditch. All three of them crawled as close as possible under the blanketing leaves of one of the many clumps of bush, and endeavoured to remain totally silent. Mannering was trembling and caused the leaves to rustle, but then he lay still. Larren and Caroline lay flat, touching cheek to cheek, and Larren could feel her hair brushing his face.

More soldiers emerged on to the path, all with fixed bayonets and stabbing haphazardly at the surrounding greenery. The carpet of pine needles that covered the dusty soil of the gardens crunched and crackled noisily under the tramping boots. They called softly to each other, grinning and enjoying the hunt. There was another rustle from the pines and Mahmud emerged, grim and resplendent in his smart uniform. The starlight struck dully on the buttons of his jacket and from the barrel of the revolver in his hand. He stood uncertainly in the centre of the path, pursing his lips, and then tugging at his moustache with his free hand. He turned as he heard another sound behind him, and an identical uniform and peaked cap appeared from the darkness beneath the trees. Larren stiffened as he recognized Korovin.

The Russian moved slowly, and the dark cruel face was drawn with pain and tight-lipped. There was still dark bloodstains in his hair just above the ear, and clearly he had not yet had time to get properly cleaned up after being pulled from the wreck of the crashed police car. He was breathing heavily as he stood by Mahmud, but although he looked ill there was another revolver gripped steadily in his hand.

They held a brief conference. Korovin's voice was harsh, sick with pain but determined. Mahmud answered crisply but coldly, gesturing fluidly with his hands. There was antagonism between the two men, and both were working hard to restrain their tempers. However, Korovin's will was stronger and his demands were enforced. Mahmud turned and barked orders into the night and there was an abrupt flurry of movement. The majority of the soldiers hurried smartly away through the pines. Two others ran to join Mahmud, who led them towards the ruined mosque, and only Korovin was left. The Russian gazed up at the great ruined tower to his right, and then went slowly towards it. As he turned the starlight struck a gleam from the pair of heavy field glasses that rested against his chest, dangling from a leather strap around his neck.

Larren watched closely, but his mind was baffled as he tried to define what was happening. Obviously there had been a difference of opinion on how the search should be conducted, and it seemed that Korovin had achieved his own way. But the soldiers had now vanished and on the face of it the search had been called off, apart from Mahmud and the two men investigating the mosque. It didn't make sense.

Korovin reached the base of the ruined tower and waited. Another half-minute passed and Larren could feel the silent movement of Caroline breathing beside him. Close behind Mannering stirred, but then became still once more. Korovin was leaning against the tower and did not straighten up until one of Mahmud's soldiers made a breathless reappearance from the pines. Then the Russian holstered his revolver and accepted an object offered by the soldier. The Russian tested it by switching on a narrow beam of light, and Larren realized that the soldier had been sent back to the cars to fetch a torch.

Korovin's next move was another puzzle. He thrust the torch into the wide leather belt of his uniform, and then helped by the soldier he climbed up over the shoulder of the base of the great tower behind him. The base was perhaps ten feet high, but once over the shoulder the Russian waved away the anxious soldier, and the man picked up his rifle and hurried off through the pines to join his comrades. Korovin turned to face the tower, and for the first time Larren noticed that there was a steel-runged ladder fixed to the brickwork, leading upwards for another twenty feet to a dark entrance hole into the tower itself. Korovin climbed the ladder and vanished inside the tower.

Caroline breathed softly.

"What the devil is he playing at? Why the field glasses and the torch? And what does he expect to find inside the tower?"

Larren said slowly:

"I think I know. From the top of the tower he'll have an excellent vantage point, with the field glasses he'll be able to see for miles, and by signalling with the torch he can direct Mahmud and his men down here. He's sent the soldiers to cordon off these gardens while he gets in position. Once he's sure that we haven't broken out he can then order them to close in again towards the centre. He's taking absolutely no chances that we might slip through his fingers again."

Mannering wriggled up to lay close beside them. He had overheard Larren's low tones and now he said wretchedly:

"We're trapped. I keep telling you it's no use. Why don't we give ourselves up?"

Caroline forestalled any response by Larren by ignoring the interruption. She said hopefully:

"What about the mosque. Perhaps we can get inside once Mahmud has searched and declared it clean?"

Larren shook his head.

"It's no good. Korovin's too smart and so is Mahmud. Those two soldiers Mahmud took with him will be posted inside the mosque once it's been checked. Then Mahmud will direct a thorough search of the gardens with Korovin watching for any breakout from above." He paused, and then finished quietly: "There's only one chance for us now."

There was a finality in his tone that caused Caroline to look sharply into his face. His eyes gleamed faintly and he was staring up at the tower.

"Simon — " She shook her head. "You're not fit."

Larren smiled. "You saw the way he climbed up into the tower, we were both in the same car crash, and I calculate that we're still fairly well matched. Korovin has been our nemesis all along. It's his relentless fanaticism that's been the driving force of our pursuit. Those two KGB men who accompanied him from Tashkent are both out of the picture now, and without Korovin I think Captain Mahmud would fold up and make an orderly retreat. Perhaps those fake charges are genuinely being pressed against us in Kabul, but Mahmud still isn't happy about co-operating too openly with Korovin. The very fact that Korovin has to be here despite his condition indicates that Mahmud won't play whole-heartedly without direct control. Eliminate Korovin and that control will be broken, then we may have a fighting chance."

Caroline hesitated a second, and then said:

"All right. But I'm more capable at the moment. I'll go."

She started to rise, the Stetchkin automatic gripped firmly in her hand, but Larren held fast to her arm.

"The gun is no use. It has to be

done silently or we'll simply bring the soldiers rushing back to the tower. And anyway, this is my kind of job. I'm still Korovin's equal. You can come as far as the tower and help me up to the foot of that ladder."

Caroline stared at him doubtfully. She had the courage to argue but the sense to know that there was no time. Then after a moment she nodded.

They rose to their feet and hurried swiftly to the base of the tower. Mannering faltered, and then came after them, reluctant to remain alone. He and Caroline combined their resources to help Larren climb up to the shoulder of the base, and despite dislodging a handful of loose bricks which almost dashed out Caroline's brains, Larren was able to reach the foot of the steel ladder. Both Caroline and Mannering hastily retreated before any more debris showered down upon their heads, and watched him from a safe distance.

Larren started up the steel ladder. It was dangerously loose and shaking, and the first half-dozen rungs were completely missing. Larren gripped the sides and leaned back to walk up the crumbling face of the brickwork, and the weight on his chest caused more vicious stabs of pain. He was relieved when he reached the first rung and could straighten his body and shift some of his weight to his legs. He was vividly conscious of the fact that he was now in full view of anyone who might glance towards the tower, and he scrambled up quickly into the dark entrance hole above him. Once there he stepped warily into the pitch blackness and waited.

There was no sound, either from above or below. No hostile eyes had witnessed that first frantic scramble, and from here on the ascent continued inside the tower. On the ground below Caroline listened tensely with the automatic in her hand, and then indicated to Mannering that they should return to their hiding place and wait.

Larren drew a deep breath and moved tentatively deeper into the tower. Total darkness enveloped him as he moved away from the entrance, but by feeling for the walls on either side he discovered that he was at the foot of a narrow spiral staircase that wound its way upwards. The brickwork of the steps had crumbled away to leave a steep, broken slope and once round the first bend he had to grope his way blindly. He had to tread carefully to prevent the uncertain surface from twisting his ankles, and several times he gritted his teeth to stop a hiss of pain as he banged his aching knee in the darkness.

He climbed steadily higher, circling round and round inside the giant tower. Occasionally there were narrow slits in the outer wall, but the faint starlight failed to penetrate, and not once did he see anything of his surroundings. He had to find his way by feel and touch alone. Several times he dislodged more broken stones which tumbled away into the blackness of the pit behind him, and he could only pray that the rattling sound would not alert Korovin above.

The climb itself began to drain his strength, for it was a long way to the top, and twice he was forced to rest.

He did not suffer from claustrophobia, but each time it was a relief to linger by one of the vertical slits in the outer wall. On the first occasion he could see down into the gardens, where the crumbling dome of the ruined mosque thrust above the tops of the trees far below. The second time he stopped the slit faced north, and he could see four more of the monstrous towers forming a square pattern that had presumably contained an even larger mosque some time in the far-distant past. Now only the corner towers remained. A thousand years of history had passed them by as they stoutly withstood the ravages of time.

Tiring, Larren climbed on. His chest hurt and his knee was giving increasing trouble, and he hoped that Korovin had suffered at least as badly. His progress became slower as he calculated that he was nearing the end of the climb, but still the winding slope of the ruined staircase spiralled interminably higher. There was a flutter and a squeak that almost startled him into falling backwards, and his heart raced as either a bird or a bat fluttered past his face, unseen in the stygian gloom. Then, when he had almost given up hope, there was a faint glimmer of relief above him.

Slowly now, inch by inch, and taking absolute care where he placed his feet, Larren moved up into the starlight. There was a roof to the tower, but at the top of the staircase were four openings in the walls that faced in each of the four main directions. The silhouette of a man stood in one of those openings, the field glasses held close to his eyes as he searched the gardens far below. He was silent and almost motionless, his legs braced apart and the upper part of his body turning slowly to follow the movement of the field glasses. Korovin was a perfect target.

Larren had to resist the impulse to destroy his enemy with one violent push. Korovin would be killed as he struck the ground below, but not before he had uttered a long, shrieking scream during the hundred-foot drop to the waiting earth. The job had to be done more silently than that.

On the last crumbling step Larren's

foot slipped, and a handful of stones clattered down inside the tower. Korovin dropped the field glasses from his eyes and wheeled with a start of alarm. His mouth gaped and he tottered back on the very edge of the fearsome drop, but Larren could not afford to let him fall. He sprang desperately forward and caught hold of the Russian's flailing arm, and then he heaved backwards and they tumbled together down the black interior of the tower.

Korovin gave a choking yell as they crashed and slithered down the broken slope of the steps, but the sounds they made were muffled now by the thick tower walls. Larren clung tightly to his opponent lest he should lose him for ever in the pitch blackness, and they crashed repeatedly into the close walls as the momentum of their fall bounced them downwards. An avalanche of broken bricks showered around them, together with an invisible cloud of fine brick dust that clogged their nostrils and stung into their already blinded eyes. At one point they were sliding head foremost down the tower, and then their progress stopped abruptly as they struck a more level section of the staircase.

Both men had been savagely battered and bruised by the fall. Both were cruelly winded and all but helpless with the excruciating agony from their earlier injuries, and both knew that they were fighting for their lives and that one of them had to die. Korovin had recognized Larren in that fleeting moment before he had been dragged inside the tower, and after his first outcry he fought silently. Neither man had any breath to spare.

Larren still held the Russian's arm, and in the darkness he struggled blindly to transfer his grip to the other's throat. Both men had been trained in every art of killing, but here the arts were useless and they were reduced to an unseeing, basic savagery. There was no room for any finesse, and pain blotted out any clear thinking. They were both weak, both grunting and gasping, and choking on the foul brick dust, and then Larren succeeded in getting both hands around Korovin's throat. In the same moment he felt the Russian's hands fasten around his own neck, the iron thumbs forcing beneath his chin which he tried to keep lowered to his chest. In identical moves each man dug his thumbs around the other's windpipe, and then they overbalanced and were crashing helplessly down and around the inside of the tower once more.

Larren was dying. The savage punishment he received as they rolled and fell were barely noticeable as the blood thundered through his brain and his bursting lungs strained in agony against the hot cage of his bruised ribs. Korovin was gouging out his wind-pipe with sharp-edged thumbs and savagely choking him to death. His own strangle-hold seemed to be having no effect, and Korovin was undoubtedly the stronger. Larren's brain reeled, the blackness was ready to descend within as well as without, and with one final grab for life he yanked the Russian's face towards his own. Their foreheads met with a stunning crack and it was Korovin's grip that faltered and failed. Larren had almost knocked himself unconscious, but a mouthful of dust and air gave him fresh strength as Korovin's hands broke away. Their tumble stopped as they cannoned into a sharp corner of the outer wall caused by one of the fissures narrowing into an open window slit, and Larren used the last of his strength to bang the Russian's head hard against the wall. Korovin went limp but Larren hung on to his strangle-hold until he was sure the Russian was dead. The avalanche of bricks and dust still rained about him, and when it stopped he collapsed beside the man he had killed and lay just as still.

★ ★ ★

Five minutes passed before he could move, and then at last he managed to stand erect. He swayed and leaned against the wall, his brain still spinning and a red mist still lingering before his eyes. Then he turned and made his way back to the top of the tower, stumbling and crawling, but at last emerging into starlight.

He stood unsteadily in the opening where he had surprised Korovin and looked down. The field glasses would have been useful, but he had heard the glass shatter during the fall down the tower so he had not bothered to retrieve them from the body. He could not distinguish anything through the canopy of pines below, but he knew that Mahmud and his soldiers would be cordoning the gardens and waiting for a signal from above. Korovin's torch lay in a niche in the brickwork, and Larren carefully picked it up.

He licked the dust from his dried lips and hoped that there had been no elaborate arrangement of signals. Then he switched on the bright beam of the torch. He pointed the beam towards the south-east, then pointed it down into the gardens and made vigorous sweeping movements again towards the south-east. The signal was an easy one to interpret, and he relaxed with a sigh of relief when he saw faint indications of movement along the outer edges of the pine trees far below. Faintly he heard the sound of Mahmud's voice shouting orders, and he knew that this time his gamble had succeeded. The cordion was breaking and the soldiers were hurrying to the south-east, led by Mahmud and with the firm conviction that the fugitives had broken out of the gardens and were escaping in that direction.

Larren turned away and fought against the overpowering pain and weakness that wanted his muscles to collapse as he started to descend the tower.

20

The Black Queen

Caroline watched as the dim figure of a man emerged from the black hole that gave entry into the ruined tower, and experienced a flush of almost painful relief as she recognized that it was Larren and not Korovin. It had been a long, nerve-racking wait. Cramp had attacked her body as she lay in hiding and her mouth was dry, but now she wanted to smile. The smile faded quickly and her anxiety rushed back as she saw the slow, fumbling way in which Larren lowered himself on to the ladder that descended the last twenty feet of the tower to the base. His movements were excruciatingly slow and it was clear that his strength was spent. He came down as though death itself was already numbing his soul.

Caroline wriggled out from the clump of bushes that concealed her, and like a nervous lap-dog Mannering followed. There was no sign or sound from Captain Mahmud and his squad of Afghani soldiers, but even so Mannering was shivering in the warm night. They reached the foot of the tower and waited. Caroline stared upwards, and in her anguish she shared the pain and torment contained in each of Larren's faltering steps down the ladder. He reached the final rung and then slipped down the last stage where the lower rungs were missing, landing heavily on the shoulder of the base but still gripping the steel side of the ladder to prevent himself from falling any farther. She heard his involuntary gasp of pain, and then he crawled to the edge of the base immediately above her.

Mannering was looking uncertainly around the now deserted gardens, and seemed startled when Caroline thrust the big Stetchkin automatic into his hand. She turned back to the tower and ignored the rain of bricks and dust that accompanied Larren as he slithered on his belly over the edge of the base, and caught him as he dropped down in front of her. His weight carried her backwards as he sagged in her arms, but with difficulty she retained her balance.

Larren made an effort to stand upright, and Caroline helped him to lean with his back against the tower. She was shocked as she looked into his bloodless face and the pain-haunted eyes. His clothes were torn and streaked with the reddish-brown of brick dust, and there were savage bruises on either side of his throat. She wet her dry lips and asked hesitantly:

"Korovin?"

"Finished." The answer was forced out and Larren coughed to clear the dust from his throat before he could go on. "And Mahmud and his men are on a wild-goose chase back into Herat. I signalled some false directions from the top of the tower."

He had to stop there, closing his eyes and rallying his strength. Then he continued:

"We have a chance now. I could see down into the main road from one of the window slits of the tower, and Mahmud has left only two soldiers to guard his transport. They're standing close together so that should make things easy. I'm no use to you at the moment, but you've got the automatic and they're only simple soldiers, so you should be able to manage with Mannering's help. Just cover them with the gun and let Mannering tie them up, or else we can take them with us and dump them along the road. We'll sabotage the three Jeeps and then get away in Mahmud's police car. That'll give us a breather, and time for me to recover."

Caroline nodded. "I can manage. This time it's your turn to take a rest." She turned to Mannering and reached out her hand to retrieve the Stetchkin automatic.

Mannering hesitated. His lip quivered, and then abruptly he took a step backwards. He levelled the automatic, and for the first time his pasty face showed strength instead of weakness. He glared at them and said positively:

"No."

Caroline regarded him coldly.

"Nevile, stop playing the fool. Simon may be below his best, but I'm still capable of handling the rest of this job, and you are still going to accompany us back to London."

She took a deliberate step forward but Mannering didn't falter. He lifted the Stetchkin so that it covered her heart and said harshly:

"Can't you understand. I am *not going back to London*. If I allow you to take me back I'm a dead man. I'm still working for the KGB. Korovin knew that. Possibly even Smith knows it by now. If he doesn't then he'll guess the truth if he ever reads your reports. London means death for me."

The suet-pudding face had become hard and bitter, and now Mannering did take another step backwards, moving so that he could keep both Caroline and Larren under the threat of the gun. He was close enough not to miss, and far enough away to give them no chance. He looked towards Larren and pure hatred gleamed from his eyes.

"Larren, I'm going to kill you." His voice was almost impersonal, as though only the opposite extreme could keep it from hysteria. "I hoped and prayed that Korovin would do it inside the tower, but now that he's dead I'll have to do it myself. Moscow wants you alive, but I'd rather see you dead."

Larren still needed the base of the tower against his back to prevent himself from falling, and he could do nothing. He glared and remained silent, trying to draw up reserves of strength that were simply not there.

Caroline said almost gently:

"Perhaps you'd like to explain, Nevile? We'd like to know all the facts."

Talking seemed to boost Mannering's confidence. He smiled, and Larren thought vaguely that it was the first smile he had yet seen on that stodgy face. The words came in the same tightly-controlled, impersonal tone.

"The facts are simple. When I first defected to the Russians three years ago I was acting as Smith's agent. But the KGB soon learned the truth and I had no choice but to genuinely defect and work for them. They allowed me to make my call for help when the time came because they saw it as an excellent opportunity to lure another of Smith's top agents into the Soviet Union. The whole thing was a trap for you, Larren. Korovin should have taken you in Samarkand, and it would have been another fine propaganda victory to publish in the west."

He paused, and then the bitterness began to intrude into his voice. "Things went wrong when you succeeded in getting me across the frontier into Afghanistan. I had to play along because those were my orders. I had to act as though I was still on your side and leave everything to Korovin. I knew that he would follow me all the way. I can assure you that I was highly relieved when he finally caught up with us, although I tried not to let it show. My job was to remain with you so that I could report anything of interest that you might let slip. A stool-pigeon often gets better results than an interrogator. That was why I was locked in the same cell as Miss Brand in the fortress at Herat. When you reappeared again, Larren, I almost panicked, but then I realized that it could only be a matter of time before Korovin recaptured us a second time. I gave him a clue by scrawling the words *north road* on the cell block wall while you two were ahead of me on the roof. I had to do it quickly with a scrap of pencil that was in my jacket pocket, but it was enough to speed up the pursuit."

"You're a clever little bleeder."

Larren spoke sarcastically. He still needed the tower for support, but he had to make the effort to speak and fill the pause. Caroline had started to edge gingerly to her left, and Mannering had to be needled and distracted. Larren went on:

"I don't suppose Korovin told you that he considered you useless. You've changed sides so many times that you're just a stink in everybody's nostrils. You say that you're going to kill me, but if the KGB wants me alive they won't be very pleased about that. Your Russian friends have seen enough of you, Mannering. You might have done better by returning to London, and taking your chances with Smith."

Mannering shook his head.

"No, Larren. London is the worst place for me. Even if Smith doesn't suspect the truth he'll be expecting information, and I haven't any. I've nothing to take back for the simple reason that the Russians didn't allow me access to anything of importance. They didn't trust me that far. That's why I dare not return to — "

Caroline had circled closer and to the left, moving imperceptively until she was within reach and yet out of the direct line of his vision, but she left her final move just a fraction too late. Mannering sensed his danger and turned swiftly to face her. His build-up of confidence evaporated with a rush, and his face took on its pasty, frightened look again. He said savagely:

"You cunning little bitch!"

Caroline stepped back, her face tense and pale. The retreat was ignored. Mannering's nerve had failed and he raised the big Stetchkin automatic. His knuckle whitened on the trigger to slam a bullet into Caroline's heart, and Larren was still as useless as a shop-window dummy and incapable of doing anything to prevent the cold-blooded murder.

In the same moment there was a faint disturbance from the deep shadow beneath the nearest pine trees. The sound that broke the stillness was not the violent crack of the Stetchkin but the soft "*phutt*" sound of a gun fitted with a silencer. Mannering's mouth sagged open and he staggered back as though an invisible sledgehammer had been swung hard against his chest. His body twisted and his dying eyes stared silently at Larren for a moment, and then his legs crumpled and he collapsed in an untidy heap to the earth. He landed on his face, but as he fell Larren saw the neat bullet hole in the left breast of his jacket.

Caroline recovered first and made a move towards the Stetchkin that had tumbled from Mannering's fingers. Three vague shapes detached themselves from the thick shadows beneath the pines and moved forward, and again Caroline froze into stillness. Wisely she drew back from the gun.

Larren watched as two men and a girl

emerged from the darkness. In each right hand was a levelled Browning P-35, and each automatic was equipped with the long fat nose of a silencer. The man who had killed Nevile Mannering was big and heavy, and wearing a thick sheepskin coat. The younger couple who supported him wore jeans and anoraks, and the man had a short, full beard. Even the girl looked grim, and they formed a menacing trio in the night.

Caroline was staring at the burly, red-faced man who had appeared first. If the expression were softened and a touch of cheerfulness added the man might have been mistaken for a typical English farmer, and it was clearly a face that Caroline had seen before. She said unbelievingly:

"Benson! What on earth — "

The big man said curtly:

"Later, Carol. Korovin — where is he?"

The name Benson had rung a bell, and to Larren the rugged, florid face also became vaguely familiar. A dim memory stirred and he knew that he had seen

Benson just once before. The big man was another of Smith's agents.

However, for the moment neither of them could answer. Benson showed a trace of impatience and repeated sharply:

"Vaslav Semonyvich Korovin, a top KGB man. He's been chasing you all across Afghanistan. Where is he now?"

"Dead." Larren spoke slowly. "I killed him. Inside the tower." Syllables and broken sentences were all he could muster.

"Dead?" It was Benson's turn to show disbelief. "You bloody fool, Larren. We wanted him alive. The whole purpose of *Strikefast* was to take Korovin alive!"

Larren was beginning to realize that Mannering was not the only one who had double-crossed him, and cold anger gave him some of the strength he needed. He said harshly:

"If you know more about *Strikefast* than I do, then you'd better start drawing me a picture. What the hell has Smith been playing at? And where do you fit in?"

Benson hesitated, but he had to accept

that Korovin was dead and after a moment he lowered the Browning P-35. His companions followed his lead like a well-trained team and some of the tension was relaxed. Benson said grimly:

"I guess you're entitled to know. When Mannering passed out that message that he was ready to come home Smith was pretty sure that he had gone over to the Reds. He knew that he was being invited to send an agent into a trap, but Smith has a mind that works in devious ways. He calculated that if he could spring the trap and get away with the bait he could lure a top KGB man into Afghanistan in pursuit. That way he could turn the trap on its originators. So he chose you to go into Samarkand and pull Mannering out. He holds you in high regard and he was pretty sure that you could do it. At the same time he arranged for me to be standing by in Kabul to take care of Korovin when he followed. We didn't know then, of course, that we were going to be lucky enough to get Korovin, but we expected somebody in that top class. Smith even leaked the fact that you had left London to make sure that the KGB launched some worthwhile opposition."

"That was nice of him," Larren cut in sourly. "And no doubt he forgot to tell me about all this in case I was a little less certain of my own capabilities. I might have decided not to go."

Benson smiled wryly. "You're getting the picture. Even Carol didn't know. We preferred to let you think that you were out on your own. However, my job was to take Korovin in Kabul, or, whoever, appeared in his place. I had Steve and Jill to help me, and the basic idea was to ship Korovin to New Delhi as diplomatic air freight. We had a trunk fixed up so that a man could be securely strapped inside, suitably drugged to keep him quiet *en route*. It's not a new trick, but even though the Egyptians made it public by bungling one of their shipments from Rome airport some time back we reasoned that it was still workable for this part of the world. It's one of those fact-being-stranger-than-fiction episodes which nobody expects to be repeated, and we're a damn sight more efficient than the Egyptians."

"So damned efficient that you couldn't resolve the whole job in Kabul," Larren countered. His anger was only just under control, and its rise was matched by the recovery of his strength. He was able to step away from the tower that supported him as he demanded: "How did you follow us here to Herat?"

"I'll admit things went wrong at Kabul. We didn't expect you to get out of the city so fast. However, we knew that you were heading south to Khandahar. Caroline passed that fact on to the British Embassy. We do have a contact there."

Larren turned sharply towards Caroline. She met his gaze without flinching and nodded slowly.

"That's true, Simon. I found time for a telephone call when I drove out alone so that we could switch cars along the Logar valley. I'd been told to make reports, but I assumed that they were being relayed through diplomatic channels to Smith in Whitehall. My briefing had insisted that I keep quiet about the progress reports, and after the job started I assumed that this was a precaution in case you were picked up in Samarkand. Obviously Smith wouldn't want the name of our man at the Embassy forced out of you by the Russians. That's why I didn't tell you that I had a link with the Embassy."

Benson nodded approvingly. "You did right. The Embassy contact tipped me off that you were headed south, and I knew that Korovin would be sufficiently organized to keep track of you and follow. So we came south on your trail. We guessed that you would try to cross the frontier into Pakistan, but at the frontier post we found you hadn't made the crossing."

Caroline said flatly:

"We ran into an ambush that turned us back."

"You should have tried again." Benson tried not to sound superior. "We encountered nothing so they must have cleared the road after they had flushed you back into Afghanistan. Anyway, we knew that you had not passed us on the road back to Kabul, and so we turned around and drove through Khandahar.

Steve speaks a small amount of pushtu, so we stopped at a roadside *chai* house on the way out and made some enquiries. An old man sitting outside remembered a black car with four people inside going past some time before us, and so we followed you to Herat. We knew that when we eventually caught up with you we would also find Korovin. In Herat we found that there was a flap taking place, and guessed that somehow you were the cause. We cruised around the streets hoping to learn something positive, and eventually found the small convoy parked outside these gardens. We dealt with the two soldiers left on guard and then came to find out exactly what was happening. I saw Mannering about to put a bullet into Carol and so I fired first."

There was a long moment of silence, and then Larren said bitterly:

"So it was all for nothing. The operation was bungled because Korovin is dead when he was wanted alive. And I was nothing but a blind pawn in the whole stinking set-up!"

Benson reflected for a moment, and

then shook his head.

"I wouldn't say that. Compare *Strikefast* to a game of chess and Mannering was the only pawn. He was worthless and might have been sacrificed by either side at any time. To draw an exact parallel, you and Korovin were the kings. One of you had to fall and be the prize to bring the game to a close."

"And I suppose you were the white knight." Larren's tone would have made acid taste sweet. "With your two noble bishops in support."

Benson made another wry smile.

"Not exactly, Larren. I prefer to think of myself as the black queen. More freedom of movement, and better control of the board."

★ ★ ★

There was nothing more to be said, and finally all five of them moved away from the pine-shaded gardens. Larren's limp was even more crippling than before, and he had to rely on Caroline's help. Parked in the road outside, some distance behind the convoy of silent Jeeps and Mahmud's police car, was a travel-stained Dormobile van, and as they approached the painted slogans were still readable on its sides. *The Three Must Get Theirs, Which Way Is East?* and *Kabul Or Bust!* The girl, Jill, opened the back doors and helped Larren and Caroline inside, while Benson heaved his burly frame into the cab behind the wheel. Steve had lingered to play swift sabotaging tricks with the engines of Mahmud's convoy, and there was a brief delay until he caught them up. Jill shifted on to the engine to let him have the front seat, and then Benson started the Dormobile and drove swiftly back into Herat.

The big man was confident that he could make a fast return trip to Khandahar and then over the frontier into Pakistan without too much trouble now that Korovin was dead. Mahmud was immobilized and it was unlikely that the Police Captain would start flashing telephone messages to have them stopped. That would incriminate him further as a tool of the KGB and it was more likely that he would be busy in covering up his own tracks and finding suitable explanations for his superiors. In any case, Larren was content to let Benson do the worrying.

He lay back with his head thankfully cradled in Caroline's lap and with his eyes closed. Operation *Strikefast* had been a failure, and what was worse it had wasted the lives of two good men. Larren thought of Smith, sitting like a paunchy, ice-brained spider in his Whitehall lair, and wondered how the little man would explain away the deaths of Sardar Sharif and Ray Gastoni to the CIA. Larren could see no justification and neither, he hoped, would the Americans. He made a fervent wish that they would give Smith hell.

THE END

Other titles in the
Linford Mystery Library:

A GENTEEL LITTLE MURDER
Philip Daniels

Gilbert had a long-cherished plan to murder his wife. When the polished Edward entered the scene Gilbert's attitude was suddenly changed.

DEATH AT THE WEDDING
Madelaine Duke

Dr. Norah North's search for a killer takes her from a wedding to a private hospital.

MURDER FIRST CLASS
Ron Ellis

Will Detective Chief Inspector Glass find the Post Office robbers before the Executioner gets to them?

A FOOT IN THE GRAVE
Bruce Marshall

About to be imprisoned and tortured in Buenos Aires, John Smith escapes, only to become involved in an aeroplane hijacking.

DEAD TROUBLE
Martin Carroll

Trespassing brought Jennifer Denning more than she bargained for. She was totally unprepared for the violence which was to lie in her path.

HOURS TO KILL
Ursula Curtiss

Margaret went to New Mexico to look after her sick sister's rented house and felt a sharp edge of fear when the absent landlady arrived.

THE DEATH OF ABBE DIDIER
Richard Grayson

Inspector Gautier of the Sûreté investigates three crimes which are strangely connected.

NIGHTMARE TIME
Hugh Pentecost

Have the missing major and his wife met with foul play somewhere in the Beaumont Hotel, or is their disappearance a carefully planned step in an act of treason?

BLOOD WILL OUT
Margaret Carr

Why was the manor house so oddly familiar to Elinor Howard? Who would have guessed that a Sunday School outing could lead to murder?

THE DRACULA MURDERS
Philip Daniels

The Horror Ball was interrupted by a spectral figure who warned the merrymakers they were tampering with the unknown.

THE LADIES
OF LAMBTON GREEN
Liza Shepherd

Why did murdered Robin Colquhoun's picture pose such a threat to the ladies of Lambton Green?

CARNABY
AND THE GAOLBREAKERS
Peter N. Walker

Detective Sergeant James Aloysius Carnaby-King is sent to prison as bait. When he joins in an escape he is thrown headfirst into a vicious murder hunt.

MUD IN HIS EYE
Gerald Hammond

The harbourmaster's body is found mangled beneath Major Smyle's yacht. What is the sinister significance of the illicit oysters?

THE SCAVENGERS
Bill Knox

Among the masses of struggling fish in the *Tecta's* nets was a larger, darker, ominously motionless form . . . the body of a skin diver.

DEATH IN ARCADY
Stella Phillips

Detective Inspector Matthew Furnival works unofficially with the local police when a brutal murder takes place in a caravan camp.

NEATH PORT TALBOT LIBRARY AND INFORMATION SERVICES

1		25		49		73	
2		26		50		74	
3		27		51		75	
4		28		52		76	
5	7118	29		53		77	
6		30		54		78	
7		31		55		79	
8		32		56		80	
9		33		57		81	
10		34		58		82	
11		35		59		83	
12		36		60		84	
13		37		61		85	
14		38		62		86	
15		39		63		87	
16		40		64		88	
17		41		65		89	
18		42		66		90	
19		43		67		91	
20		44		68		92	
21		45		69		COMMUNITY SERVICES	
22		46		70			
23		47		71		NPT/111	
24		48		72			